THE DRAGON'S PROMISE

SILVER DRAGON SHIFTER BROTHERS 2

MARIE JOHNSTON

Penn

The only female I ever wanted was promised to my brother. But he found a woman, fell in love, and Venus was back on the market. Only she doesn't want someone like me. A self-professed nerd, but worse, a male ten years younger than her. She's stubborn, but I'm determined to win her over. Until she leaves.

Venus

The cost is high for a dragon shifter who's single after a certain age. For a girl who grew up the laughingstock of her clan, mating Penn is the best way for history to repeat itself. So I flee to live my last days in peace. Only the persistent and devastatingly handsome male finds me. And when I start to melt, another female stakes her claim. And I have to decide if shifter politics are worth losing my life and my guy over.

CHAPTER
ONE

enus

I GLARED at my oldest brother, Lachlan. "It's not funny." As if my other brother Ronan's infuriating joke would be funny the fiftieth time I heard it, but I hadn't laughed the first time he said it.

How are Venus and mountain lion shifters alike?

They're both cougars.

Lachlan's grin was wolfish. An apt enough description since dragonish wasn't a word. "Nope. I'm pretty sure it's funny."

I could almost forgive my other brother Ronan in exchange for Lachlan's smile, which he so rarely did. The humor was at my expense. My brothers' jokes usually were, but unlike our parents, they said them in private and not in front of the rest of the clan so they could join in the ridicule. I'd grown a thick skin over the years, but my current situation was new and extra raw.

I had been passed over by the male I'd been sworn to mate since I was a kid. A deal made between Jade clan's council and Silver clan's council. Many other females would've been thrilled to be paired with Deacon Silver. He was more than easy on the eyes, and as the ruler of Silver clan, he was the ruler over all dragon shifters.

But I'd been as relieved as him to be freed from obligation, and his human mate had become one of my best friends. For a female who didn't have many friends, I didn't take that lightly.

Deacon wasn't at the root of Ronan's joke. It was Deacon's youngest brother Penn who'd valiantly swooped in and offered to take his place.

I should be grateful. I had to be mated by the time I turned thirty-five. It was a critical milestone in a shifter's life. Extra critical for a kid of a ruling family. I had less than a month before my birthday and no prospects. My dating options hadn't been stellar since I'd been old enough to date, and I'd used my eventual mating to Deacon as an excuse not to foster anything long term.

I eyed the red-and-green sippy cup Ronan had set on the corner of Lachlan's desk when he told his joke. Penn was young, but not that young. Though his twenty-five years could just as well make a millennium between us instead of ten years.

I knew of one topic that would get Lachlan to clamp his mouth closed so tight he wouldn't speak for the rest of the day, and Ronan would find somewhere else to be. "Are you going to keep the cup, Lachlan? For you and Indy?"

Lachlan's gaze turned to stone in an instant. He

snapped his mouth shut and glared at me. His mate, Indy, was off-limits. And most of the time, I left the subject alone. Not too long ago, Lachlan had been in the same position as me. In the same position as Deacon had been last week. My oldest brother was the Jade clan leader. If he didn't mate by thirty-five, he'd be executed. Other shifters had a grace period, but many didn't dare wait too long. Our aggression was insidious, and at a mature age, without an anchor, it lost control too quickly. As a ruling family, we were the example for breaking the rule.

Lachlan had been a lot like Deacon, only he'd fucked his way through Jade Hills without lingering long enough in any female's bed to cause speculation about mating. Indy was younger than Ronan, and she hadn't been any different from the other females in the clan. She had succumbed to Lachlan's brooding charm, and he'd discarded her just as fast too. But then his thirty-fifth birthday had been around the corner and next thing we knew, he showed up in front of Jade's council with Indy on his arm.

As far as I knew, he hadn't cheated on her. And despite the attempts of several of the females he'd been with, he and Indy didn't seem to have an open-mate relationship. But they weren't a poster for a happy relationship either. Lachlan's temper had been worse since he mated Indy. And Indy had isolated herself in the little apartment above the clan's city hall.

Maybe someday he'd talk to me or Ronan about it. But until then, if he poked the topic of Penn, I would do the same with Indy.

"When is Penn due to arrive?" Lachlan asked in his best *I'm the leader* tone.

"I don't know, and I don't care." Yet my heart rate

kicked up. I was a female with a healthy sex drive. Attraction wasn't the problem with Penn. My past and present were.

My brothers exchanged a look. It was Ronan who spoke. "Venus, come on. The kid is saving your ass."

That was the problem. My brothers called Penn *the kid*. And Ronan was correct. Penn would be saving my ass —if I accepted his offer.

Like with Deacon, most other females would be thrilled to mate him. It wasn't just his looks with the silky dark hair that was on the shaggy side and crystal-blue eyes with the silver flecks and the irises that made them sparkle like no gem known to man when he laughed.

Penn was one of the good ones. He liked to laugh. He wasn't moody and cranky like Lachlan. Penn didn't have a perpetual serious expression like his oldest brother, Deacon. He wasn't ready to throw down at a moment's notice like Ronan, nor was he on the snidely arrogant side like his other brother Steel.

Being around him made me feel every one of my thirty-four years. I had grown up with parents who made it their goal in life to piss off the other dragon clans. Lachlan hadn't wanted to foster as much animosity since our parents had died, but he also didn't go out of his way to make friends. Our clan's reputation carried on with little effort. So, the first strike against being Penn's mate was being born into the rebellious, petulant clan that made other dragon shifters roll their eyes.

The second strike against me was Lachlan's brilliance. We went to mostly shifter schools, but they were organized as if we were regular humans. And that meant elementary school. That meant reading out loud, and doing math problems on the board, and reciting the capital of every state.

That also meant the entire class witnessing the teacher helping me pronounce simple words. Having the teacher call another student to correct the errors in my math on the board in front of the class. And enduring the laughter of all the other students when I mixed up capitals and states. I knew the capital of the state I lived in was Bismarck. Wasn't that enough?

My brothers hadn't joined in on the teasing. They beat the crap out of anyone they witnessed laughing at me. Which only made my home life hell. Our parents hadn't tolerated weakness. That included a daughter who needed her brothers to stand up for her. As it was a major detriment that I hadn't wanted to fight.

Small towns had long memories, and it was no different in shifter towns. My troubles in school would be compared to Penn's early graduation and how he'd finished his college degree by twenty only to start graduate school.

I had gone to school to be a cosmetologist. I wouldn't have been able to, but my parents had died in a house fire. Lachlan took over the lead and allowed me to go. Because that was how it worked in the shifter world.

Fifteen years of doing hair and manicures and pedicures, chatting with women who wanted to support me instead of tearing me down had been a blissful life I didn't know was possible when I was younger. And it was all going to end. Whether I mated Penn or met my fate, I was going to lose the tidy life I'd made for myself.

Part of the previous mating agreement was that I move to Silver Lake. I had no reason to think it was going to change. I would have to move, and my clients wouldn't follow me to Silver Lake thanks to clan pride and the rivalry Silver and Jade had had for generations.

My brothers were watching me. Right. We were on the topic of Penn saving me. He was due in Jade Hills soon to go over the new contract with Lachlan.

I wasn't invited.

To be fair, I wasn't *not* invited, but I also didn't want to be around. "On that note, I've gotta go."

"Got some hair to tease?" There was no bite to Lachlan's tone, and I was used to their comments about my job. I also trimmed their hair for free, so they didn't dare dog my job that much.

"The higher the hair, the closer to heaven." I left my brothers in city hall and went outside. Jade Hills city hall was in an old armory. Lachlan had remodeled the upper level before he'd mated Indy.

I had a house on the edge of town I happily decorated any damn way I wanted. The home I didn't have growing up. Ronan rented a house right by Main Street. The place we'd grown up in had been the house my parents had burned in. One of the few things that killed shifters before old age.

I shouldn't be glad they were gone—but the relief was undeniable.

Lachlan never said, but I thought he was determined to do better. It didn't help that Jade Hills was still full of the older generations. Octogenarians voiced their opinions loud and with enough bolster that younger shifters listened. My brother had his hands full. I hated to make his job more stressful.

But I was going to.

I reached my car, thankful I had put the top up. I wanted a little privacy, and with the sun arching high overhead, chasing away all the shadows, I would only receive it if I closed myself in somewhere.

I got inside and pulled up the newest number in my phone. I had made two new friends. Human friends. Which my clan would be happy to point out were the only friends I could make. But I didn't care. Ava and Avril liked and respected me when they had every reason to be catty bitches.

Ava didn't have a mean bone in her. Avril would throw down to defend the ones she loved. And that was how I had met her. She had charged into Deacon's house to rescue Ava. When she realized there was nothing wrong, she had stayed. The two humans could have spent the day together and ignored me, but it had turned into a girls' day.

Avril answered. "Oh my god, I'm glad I put your name in. I almost didn't answer."

"Hey, I'm glad you're excited to hear from me. Because I wanted to see if you were around for the next few weeks. I'd like to get away for a while."

PENN

I ROUNDED the last stretch to my house. My feet pounded the pavement and sweat trickled between my shoulder blades. Dragon shifters had a naturally high metabolism. We didn't need to work out. But I found that a solid five miles a day kept our instinctive aggression at bay. My running habit was the reason I was considered the most laid-back Silver brother.

All of us were easygoing as far as shifters were concerned. I chalked it up to our leadership roles. Good leaders weren't aggressive. They weren't hotheads who reacted instead of reflected. As the third in line to rule Silver clan, I didn't have to worry about my leadership abilities as much as my next oldest brother Steel. And now that Deacon was mated, my concerns crashed to zero. But I still liked to regulate my emotions. Especially when my pride and ego had recently taken such a massive hit.

I had to be level now more than ever. Venus didn't want some hothead. I'd heard enough stories about her parents, and she hadn't found someone else to mate beyond the contract with my brother. That had to mean she was discerning—or gun-shy.

She might not think I was serious, but I'd never wanted anything or anyone more.

Too bad I wasn't coming to her with gainful employment under my belt, but no one knew about that yet.

I kicked up the pace for the last two hundred yards.

Steel's pickup sat in front of my house. My neighbor's granddaughter, Ella, sauntered across my path. She changed her focus from a surly Steel to me. I didn't feel like chatting with Ella. She was more forward than I was used to, and with her grandmother's encouragement, she practically threw herself at me.

When she heard the pounding of my steps, she changed course to intercept me. As much as I wasn't interested in her, I couldn't blame her. Steel had been a grumpy fucker for the last week, and he refused to tell us what was going on.

"Hey, Penn. How many miles today?" Ella's vibrant grin made her appear even younger than her twenty-one years. Still in college, she'd come back to Silver Lake to spend the summer with her grandma.

Ella was everything the clan thought a guy like me should want. Gorgeous with long dark hair the color of burnished brass. She was intelligent. I heard her talking to her grandma on the front porch when she'd first arrived. She planned to apply for graduate programs in her field. Biomechanics. Ella was no slouch in the academic world.

Pretty, smart, and single. I should be all over it.

The only female I was interested in had a salty attitude, long sun-bleached tresses with dyed-green tips, and emerald eyes that saw through everyone's bullshit.

"I just did five today." I needed to take the nervous edge off before my brothers and I went to Jade Hills to do final negotiations with Lachlan Jade.

She ran her fingers through her long hair. "I told you to call me. I can be a running buddy."

I gave an easy shrug, as if I had just forgotten. I had no plans to adopt a running buddy, and if I did, it wouldn't be a single young female. I would not give Silver Lake or Jade Hills fuel for gossip or speculation. I wouldn't put it past Venus to stubbornly walk into an execution on her thirty-fifth birthday instead of mating me.

"Sorry. I usually just want to space out anyway."

Disappointment flared in her doe-brown eyes. "No problem. Grandma wants to know if you can come over tonight. My uncle brought some elk steaks."

My stomach reared its hungry head at the mention of elk meat. Ella's uncle farmed elk, and Ella's grandma had shared some with me over the last couple of years. It was good stuff, and after my morning run, I could literally eat a horse. But for the next month, I would be careful who I socialized with. I was in an uphill battle to get Venus to accept me even if I was her only option. I didn't need gossip and speculation to tank my already dismal chances.

"Thanks, but Steel and I are leaving town."

Ella glanced at Steel and took what seemed to be an involuntary step backward.

When I looked at my brother, I could see why. Angry storm clouds gathered across his face. He seemed to be ignoring us, but whatever was on his mind ate at him. What was his problem?

"Okay." Ella backed down the sidewalk toward her grandma's house. "I'll let her know. Have a good trip."

"Tell her thanks for the offer." I waved, then rounded on Steel, keeping my back to my neighbor's place. "You scared her away."

Steel blinked like I had snapped him out of a trance. He glanced from a disappearing Ella to me. "Well, it's not as if you're interested."

He didn't seem to be either. He wasn't that much older than me that Ella wouldn't be a good choice for him. But the way he was glowering at the sidewalk, I was surprised he'd noticed she was there.

"I'm not interested. I've already made my decision."

He shook his head. "When you first offered, I thought you were doing it for Deacon. You've really got it bad for her."

I dug the toe of my shoe into the concrete. "Yeah, well, it won't matter if she can't get over the age difference."

"What if it's not just the age difference?"

I scowled, not liking this line of questioning. "What do you mean?"

"What if she's just not that into you?"

Then I would have to deal with it, but I would do what I could to make sure that wasn't the case. And in order to do that, I needed to be around her. Venus had a knack for avoiding me. If she was around me, it was always with other people.

Ordinarily, I'd respect that space. If she didn't like me, she didn't like me. Except her life was on the line. Unless she was in love with someone else, I at least wanted her to get to know me before she made a decision that could cost her everything.

The whole point of this contract negotiation was to give her a chance to get to know me. I had made it seem as if I was asking Deacon's approval to go to Jade Hills. Either we thought alike, or he knew me better than I thought. He'd already arranged a meeting.

"All right. Go shower before we take off. I don't need your scent all over me. Save it for Venus."

Her scent was imprinted in my brain. She smelled sweet, like white chocolate coating on ice cream—the stuff that hardens when exposed to air. Kind of like the shifter herself. I wanted to know if she was soft and molten in private.

"Be out in ten."

Before I walked into my house, he said, "How long are we staying?"

Until I won her over. "She has over three weeks before her birthday. Might take that long for her to follow through." If she followed through. My gut churned. I didn't want her beautiful life snuffed out. For me, and for Jade clan. They seemed to be in a period of recovery since Lachlan had taken over, and if he had to terminate his sister for breaking one of our most critical rules, the entire clan might suffer.

"Don't you have to teach or something?"

Or something. "The semester is done." And my teaching contract was not renewed. Humiliation burned through me, but I shoved it away. I'd deal with it later.

My phone buzzed. I slipped it from my pocket. Deacon's name ran across the screen. "Hey. Steel and I were about to take off."

"You might need to change plans," Deacon said. "She's gone."

CHAPTER

TWO

enus

I STEERED THROUGH TRAFFIC, following the robotic directions pouring out of my speaker until I ended up in front of a building comprised of houses and garages that looked attached and smashed together. Condos of the city. Avril's one condo probably cost more than a new build in Jade Hills.

I parked in her driveway and ran to the door. I pressed the doorbell and twirled my sunglasses in my hand while I shifted my weight from foot to foot. Was this too impulsive? Would Lachlan track me down?

I left a note, but it wouldn't look good to run away like a rebellious little girl. Which was what I was doing under the guise of visiting a friend—an eight-hour drive away. My brothers could read between the lines, but there was a chance the council and their staff wouldn't be fooled.

My luck was usually shit, but it was worth a shot.

Avril opened the door with a grin that didn't distract from her bloodshot eyes and the messy hair that hadn't seen a comb for at least two days. She had casually mentioned she was single, but she hadn't mentioned she was devastated. "Venus!"

I wrapped her in a hug. There was no use pointing out her haggard appearance as a greeting. "I can totally get a hotel if this is a bad time."

"No." She blinked. Then she blinked again. She lost the battle against an onslaught of tears that spilled down her cheeks. "I'm alone anyway."

I hugged her again. Breakups sucked no matter the species, though I had no real experience. Between my "bad attitude" and my expectations of not being treated like crap, short term was all I could get. It hadn't bothered me. My single-girl life rarely did, but now I was dangerously single.

"It might be too soon to admit"—I held Avril at arm's length—"but are you better off without him?"

Tears rolled down her cheeks as she thought about my question. Her face crumpled. "Yes."

I pulled her back into my embrace. If she had the wherewithal to answer honestly, then the source of Avril's emotions was regret. She'd spent too long with a man that deep down she knew wasn't good for her. She'd wasted her time, and acknowledging it could be harder than a broken heart.

A girl learned a few things behind the salon chair.

"It still sucks." I dropped my overnight bag on the floor. I had three weeks' worth of luggage in my trunk.

"But now I know that we're also going to celebrate a massive douche weight loss."

Avril chuckled and sniffled. She pushed her hair off her face. "You're right. I lost the best kind of weight. The kind that always made me feel like I was an inconvenience. That liked to point out I wasn't the priority I thought I should be in his life. And especially a massive ton of weight that blamed me for not being able to orgasm before twenty minutes of *work*."

All of that was awful, but the orgasm shame was like the cherry on top of what sounded like a bad relationship. "Glad I could help put it into perspective."

"I've already bawled on the phone to Ava, but it's different now that she's not here. A visit is just what I needed." She shook herself like she could fling her grief off. We were on a split landing and she went to the stairs that led to the lower level. "I'll show you to your room."

I followed her down the plush taupe carpet to a cozy, homey basement that was staged like it could be put on the market next week. Cushy couch and recliner. Entertainment center. Fake fireplace. She'd probably purchased the condo with family on her mind while her ex strung her along. Several of my clients had told the same stories over the years. "Thanks for letting me crash on short notice."

"Of course. I was delighted. I messaged Ava to tell her in case she could get away, but you know, she's still in the honeymoon stage."

So my departure had reached Deacon. It was safe to assume that Penn knew I'd left. How would he take the rejection?

My pulse stuttered. He was a nice guy, and I'd ditched him. But facing him, with his expressive blue eyes and that mouth that liked to say things that got under my skin, made it hard to assemble my thoughts around him.

Avril walked into a simple guest bedroom not unlike a hotel room. Thanks to the garden level, the window was larger than a normal basement window. The blinds were a neutral shade of brown, the bedding was different shades of neutral, and the carpet's color was just as bland.

As uneventful as the decorating style was, it was nicer than anything I'd grown up with. Nothing matched in my house and I preferred it—it had character. I'd been around humans enough to know that I grew up the equivalent of trailer trash despite being born to a ruling family of dragon shifters.

I dropped my bag on the bed and sank onto the mattress next to it. Avril was nursing a broken heart, and I wasn't here for a relaxing vacay. If Avril had treated me like anything less than a friend after knowing me for such a short amount of time, I probably wouldn't say anything, but she was a friend and I didn't want to dupe her.

"I need to tell you something."

She leaned against the door frame and folded her arms across her chest. "You're not here for manicure parties and shopping sprees?"

"I packed my manicure travel kit—pedicure too, so that's not ruled out." I couldn't afford a shopping spree. Dragons and their hoards weren't just a myth, however my family burned through their hoard long ago and didn't participate in human activities like investing, leaving a legacy of being broke as hell. "I want to visit you. Please don't think I don't want to hang out with you."

Avril's expression brimmed with support. "I'm honored you turned to me when something's wrong." She sat beside me, her body cocked toward me.

I told her the human-friendly version of what I was going through. "You know how Ava told you that Deacon and I were engaged?"

"That your families had this idea about how you two could kind of grow up together and get married? Like an arranged marriage?"

Ava had already taken care of the bulk of the story. "Well, when he broke off our engagement to mate— marry Ava, they were afraid my family would get upset. So Penn offered to take his place."

"Penn's hot," Avril said in a clinical way that said she had zero interest in him. "But looks aren't everything when it comes to spending your life with someone."

With Penn, looks could be everything. Those blue eyes that turned to different shades, depending on his mood. My favorite was playful blue. His irises lightened to the blue of an early spring day. I hadn't seen him angry, but I could imagine that they changed to the gray of a fall storm. But enough about his looks. That wasn't helping.

"He's twenty-five."

Avril nodded, waiting for me to continue.

Right. She was his age. I poked my sternum. "I'm almost thirty-five."

She nodded like she was waiting for me to tack on more reasons being with Penn was a bad idea. Her mouth formed an O. "I see. That's your issue with him?"

I jumped up and started pacing the room, pinging from wall to wall like a hot mess of a Ping-Pong game.

"Yes, it's a bad thing. Ten years younger than me? Ten years."

"So, just to get this straight, it's you that has a problem with his age and not your family?"

Step, step, turn. Step, step, turn. The room wasn't very wide and my strides lengthened when I was upset. "My family doesn't have an issue with it per se, but they would give me eternal shit about it. The entire clan—town would. 'Look at Venus. She had to get a guy who doesn't know how stupid she is to mate with her.'"

"All they're concerned about is procreating?"

I realized I had said mate. "I meant marry, sorry."

"Oh." Avril tapped her chin and mumbled, "I don't think anyone would look at Penn, Steel, or Deacon and think you're settling. I can't imagine anyone thinking Penn wouldn't deserve you."

"Jade Hills is different. It's a small town."

"No need to say more. I get it. Small towns can be brutal."

I didn't know what her story was, and she didn't offer more. I took a seat next to her again. "I didn't have a good reputation growing up. My dad and my mom were kind of like the mayor and the police chief of Jade Hills. So it was extra embarrassing for them when teachers had to cheat on my grades to get me through school. I struggled with almost every subject and had a bad attitude. I'm not exactly seen as a great catch."

"You are a great catch, but why do you even have to be caught? If you don't want to get married, why can't you just stay single?"

And that was where the human-friendly version failed. "I can't *not* get married. There's a deep and break-able family tradition of being married by the time we're thirty-five. And because of who I am, I can't break it without serious consequences."

Her expression turned distraught. "They'll make you leave your home?"

Since I wouldn't be here in a month to explain why I died, I just nodded.

"Well, you can come live here. Stay with me."

Tears burned the backs of my eyes. Her sweet offer meant so much to me. "I wish it was that easy. I'll lose everything."

It was her turn to comfort me. She wrapped her arms around my neck and rested her head on my shoulder. "I feel this strong urge to talk you into being with Penn. He's handsome, and I know I wasn't around him long, but he seems really cool. But you shouldn't be forced to be with someone you don't want to be with. You shouldn't be forced to be with anyone."

I wanted to be with someone. I wanted to have a relationship. Someone I could talk to about all my thoughts and feelings. Someone I trusted not to ridicule what came out of my mouth. "Unfortunately, in my family, we need to be in a committed relationship. We tend to be crazy cat ladies—and men—if we don't settle down." We tended to eat those cats if we stayed single and went feral.

"I don't know if I have enough ice cream for our woes, but I have a lot to choose from. What kind do you like?"

I let out a moan. "Could you be more perfect? I fucking love ice cream. I don't care what flavor it is."

∿

PENN

· · ·

Jade Hills shouldn't be so much different from Silver Lake. Dragon shifters had centuries to accumulate wealth. Whether our currency came in the form of gems or bitcoin, we were a species who knew how to keep and grow money.

What had Jade Hills done with all their wealth? Our genetics might be complicated, but our living circumstances weren't. Dragon shifters lived in rural areas, places with enough space and privacy to shift without getting busted. The other shifters, wolves and mountain lions, also gravitated toward rural communities. We were part human, part beast, and the needs of the beast were critical to provide for.

Silver Lake maintained its roads, built playgrounds and schools, and provided for the needs of its members. Our cities weren't ostentatious, but they were built with quality and well maintained.

I had worried about losing a rim when I hit the first pothole after I crossed into town. It had been years since I'd come to Jade Hills. When my parents were in charge of Silver Lake, they had quit taking the three of us, fearing that having all of their heirs in one place would be too tempting for Lachlan's parents.

Steel led the way into the cold, imposing building that was city hall. Even though I was the one who agreed to meet Venus, Steel was older than me. It was a subtle sign of respect to Jade, more like an olive branch, that Lachlan was sure to notice.

There was no receptionist. No staff roaming the building. Outdated white tile lined the floor and the door frames were metal. It was every inch an old armory. I'd heard Lachlan and his mate lived on the upper level that spanned one end of the building. I hoped he'd changed the aesthetic before he'd moved his mate in.

A younger version of Lachlan reclined in a rickety wooden chair outside of the main office. Ronan. He was Steel's age, and Lachlan was older than Deacon. I couldn't do anything about her age, but I knew being so much younger than her brothers was a huge part of her issue with me.

"Lachlan, our guests have arrived." The corner of the male's mouth tipped up, falling short of a smile. His dark gaze was calculating, at odds with his relaxed posture.

Lachlan appeared in the doorway of his office, a heavy scowl weighing on his face, making him seem much older than he was. If he wasn't as tall and fit as Deacon, I'd expect him to be stooped and muttering a constant stream of complaints.

"You're early," he said in a flat tone.

"Your sister is not something I wanted to be late for." But I was too late. Was she at Avril's already? I wanted to race after her, but it was critical I finished my business with her brothers—more important that I saw for myself how they felt about this mating. Maybe they'd told her to leave.

The intense look Lachlan spared me almost made me recoil. "Your brother didn't feel the same way."

"My brother wasn't meant to be with her." I was. No one believed me, but Venus was mine. I didn't care if anyone believed it. But I thought she was going to be the hardest one to convince.

Lachlan straightened as the intensity around him closed in like a cloak. Ronan sat forward in his chair and studied me. He tipped his head toward Steel. "Why did you offer and not him?"

Steel spread his hands and flashed a deceptively good-natured smile. "Penn beat me to it."

The way the other two brothers focused on me was as if Steel had disappeared.

"And you want to change the contract our parents had drawn up how?" Suspicion dripped from Lachlan's tone. I didn't blame him. Our parents hadn't gotten along, but the council members had seen the need to unite our two clans in some way. That didn't mean Silver Lake's council made it easy on Jade Hills' council.

"You can rip up the contract. I'm only interested in being your sister's mate."

Lachlan's dark brows dropped. "I don't believe you."

"I don't care."

"My sister doesn't want to be with you."

"You want her to die?"

Both brothers flinched. I'd heard a lot about how hard life was in Jade Hills. Tempers flared quicker, and the violence was dirtier than other clans. But I'd heard my parents talk about how hard it was for Venus with her family. Had her brothers experienced the same?

I had assumed so. Their protectiveness startled me, but it made sense after the way they'd grown up. But it also meant she wanted to leave. They hadn't forced her.

Ronan peered around the room. He cocked his head as if he was listening for anyone else in the building. Our hearing was better than humans', and in this old place it would be hard for anyone to sneak up on us. Doors would squeak and steps would echo.

Still, he kept his voice low. "If you're so intent on being with my sister, why did she leave before you got here?"

Steel and I had talked about her sudden departure on

the thirty-minute drive here. Venus's disappearance wouldn't go over well with a clan like hers. Her people would see it as a weakness. She was running from a fight instead of facing one. The last thing I wanted to do was fight. The only way I wanted to raise my heart rate around her was to—

I wasn't fighting my dick's reaction around her brothers. "There's a lot of logistics to work out to keep our clans happy. I told her to get away for a while before we have to face it all."

Lachlan lifted his chin. His eyes narrowed. His nostrils were flared like he smelled my lie. Lying to a clan ruler was a punishable offense. If he called me out, or worse, wanted me to answer for it, then this thing with Venus was going to be harder than I thought. But if he went with it, that said a lot. He might not exactly be an ally, but he at the very least wanted to protect the reputation of his sister—and he wanted her to choose me instead of death. I could work with that.

Ronan was glancing between me and Lachlan. Steel folded his arms across his chest to cover any reaction to the lie I didn't talk to him about beforehand.

Lachlan waited another moment before he said, "So you know where she's at then?"

I nodded, grateful Ava told Deacon everything, and that she hadn't thought Venus was fleeing because of me.

"Then you know to tell her I'd better see her ass and your ass in here before ten a.m. on her birthday." Lachlan stepped back into his office and disappeared.

Ronan kicked back in his chair, stretching his legs out and crossing them at the ankles. "Sounds like I can tell the town the good news." His direct gaze held mine, challenging me. "You know, that you and my sister decided to go on a nice little getaway before the big day."

"Spread the news," I said with confidence I didn't feel. "I'll return with her before her birthday."

Ronan cocked that arrogant brow. "And when is that?"

"Three weeks and five days."

Respect filled his gaze, along with grudging approval. "You sure you don't want to review that contract? There's some good stuff in there for Silver Lake."

"I care more about what's good for your sister."

"Then you'd better work that Silver charisma because she's stubborn as fuck. If I have to bury my sister because of it, I'm going to take it out on you."

"I'll win her over."

He snorted. "Knowing when her birthday is doesn't mean you know. Good thing I've heard you're a quick learner."

I knew as much as I could about Venus. Ask me anything. What I didn't know was why she was so against giving me a chance.

CHAPTER

THREE

enus

AFTER A NIGHT of ice cream and murder shows, I woke up feeling less panicked than I had been the last few days. I had made the right decision about leaving. Everyone else might see it as cowardly, but I knew I needed time and space to figure out what I was going to do.

Thankfully, I had kept my schedule clear. When news of my departure spread through Jade Hills, perhaps people would notice that no one complained about me canceling their appointments. A minor detail, but it should look like I planned this trip. I'd planned the time off, not the trip.

I went upstairs and found Avril in the kitchen. She had her hair in a ponytail, workout leggings on, and was dumping various items into a blender.

"I'm going to make some noise." She shot me an apologetic look before she put the lid on and hit blend.

The whir filled the place as I ducked into the bathroom. I had already cleaned up, but that was basic hygienic stuff. Avril was up after a long night looking like she could pose for a fitness magazine. She wouldn't think that, but she had the girl-next-door beauty with the charisma people gravitated toward.

I gave myself a once-over in the mirror. Not too shabby for getting little sleep and riding on a sugar high. I had braided my hair and wrapped it around my head like a crown. My hair had been my advertising for so long, it was odd to wake up and wonder how much longer I would be styling it.

For a girl who grew up wishing I wasn't who I was, I sure didn't want to leave my life. But with my parents gone and Lachlan in charge, no one messed with me anymore. There were the looks, and the whispers, but those faded the older I got. I didn't want them returning. Mating Penn would ensure that happened.

Somehow, all my thoughts circled back to him.

In the kitchen, Avril had poured two glasses of reddish-purple slop into a mug.

"I figured we needed a transition from ice cream to solid food. Do you like blueberries and bananas and protein powder?"

I grabbed the glass and one of the spoons she set out. "I like food anyone else makes."

She chuckled, and we sat at the table. Her condo looked different during the day. The sunlight streaming through the windows made it impossible to dwell on our man troubles.

Avril crossed one leg over the other. "I don't work until tomorrow. What do you want to do today?"

"What would you do today if I weren't here?"

She wrinkled her nose and studied the thick slush in her glass. "Mope."

"So I'm not impeding on anything productive." I put a spoonful of the sweet mixture in my mouth.

"It's gorgeous out. Maybe we should go enjoy the weather."

"There's so much more to do here than in Jade Hills."

I loved my hometown. I shouldn't after the way I was treated growing up and the bad memories of my parents that still linger. But it was a beautiful part of the country. There were enough small lakes that weren't overpopulated with anglers to explore. Acres of trees. And it was remote enough that I could shift whenever I got the itch.

My clan didn't have the best reputation. I ran through the different clans in the Twin Cities area. Avril lived north of the Twin Cities, and that brought me closer to Garnet, Emerald, and Peridot.

What had my parents done to screw them over? Would they let me wander through their land and shift?

It was possible that if I ran across any dragon shifters, they wouldn't realize who I was. They'd know I was a dragon shifter, but not one of their clan.

"I haven't been to the zoo in forever." Avril swished her spoon in her glass. "Is that too childish?"

Tiny tendrils of anxiety swirled through my gut. I'd never been to a zoo. We had ranchers in our clans. Only those animals had grown up around the ranchers.

What if I got the animals riled up? Would chaos reign and it would be my fault? I could hear the whispers sprint through Jade Hills if something happened and my clan found out. They'd say five-year-old shifters knew better than to go to the zoo, but not me.

"We don't have to go," Avril said after I was silent too long.

I shook my head. "No, I'd love to go. It's just that..." I pushed my half-finished smoothie away before the rest of it curdled in my stomach. "I have a weird fear when it comes to caged animals." I feared their fear, but this was the best way to explain it.

"We could go to a park."

"A park would be safe." I rubbed my arms, trying to chase away a chill that had nothing to do with the cold breakfast. "Sorry."

"Why would you be sorry?" Avril looked genuinely baffled. "I'm not going to make you do anything you don't want to do. I want your time here to be fun, and I know you feel like you crashed my house, but you're helping me. Really. Without Ava, I would've been devastated. Ian had become my everything. I didn't realize how bad my life revolved around him until I was roaming through this place, not knowing what to do. You know what's worse?"

I shook my head.

"When you asked if I was better off—that's really stuck with me. He wasn't the nicest to me, and he was growing insidiously worse. I didn't notice, and I'm afraid I wouldn't have for a long time if it hadn't been for you."

"Ian can go fuck himself." Comforted that I wasn't being a pain in the ass, I elaborated on her park idea. "We could do a picnic."

Avril's eyes lit up. "I know just the place."

We cleaned up our breakfast. I ran to my room and grabbed my green tote bag with my sunglasses and a different pair of shoes. I waited at the landing as she gathered her items.

She charged down the stairs, a grin stretching across her face. "Let's do it. Two single girls on the loose."

Tingles exploded across my shoulders and traced down my spine. What the hell? A flush of heat started at my toes and worked its way up my body. I wouldn't let anything ruin this day with Avril. I didn't know what the reaction was for, but to cover it up, I opened the door and charged outside. Right into a broad chest.

Strong arms wrapped around me as an oomph escaped the male I had crashed into. A mix of cedar, sandalwood, and coriander circled around me, brushing away the earlier tingles and imprinting on my skin as surely as if it was tangible.

"Well, hi to you too."

That deep voice. His rumble was even worse when my hands were plastered on his chiseled chest. It took another few seconds for my brain to come online. My body was enjoying being smashed against Penn too much to care about the details of the situation.

"What are you guys doing here?" Avril sounded as incredulous as I should feel. I would get there—once I quit touching Penn.

Wait, *you guys?* Steel was behind Penn, and I hadn't even noticed. So much for my position at the top of the shifter chain. I lost all awareness around Penn.

"We're here for V," Penn said without taking his royal-blue eyes off me.

The silver shards in his irises sparked. Anger? Irritation? He hunted me down like the untamed creature I had acted like when I fled Jade Hills. He must be pissed. It didn't look good for Venus Jade to leave a Silver brother.

It didn't look good when a girl like me left one of the most eligible bachelors of my kind. "How did you find me?"

The silver in his eyes cleaned brighter as the corners of his mouth tipped up. "Oh, Venus. It wouldn't matter where you went. I would've found you."

PENN

VENUS FROZE like she didn't know whether to throw me onto the sidewalk and stomp on me or storm back into the house and slam the door in my face.

"Hey, Avril," I said to deflect the attention off Venus's dismay. "Didn't mean to crash the party."

Avril blinked and stepped out of the house beside Venus. "How did you know where she was?" She shook her head. "Never mind. I'm sorry, Venus, I wasn't thinking. I told Ava you were here, but that was before..."

Before Venus had likely told her I was pursuing her and she didn't want me to.

"It wasn't a secret," Venus mumbled in a way that told me she had wanted to stay secret.

Avril lifted her gaze past my shoulder. "Steel."

"Avril."

If Steel hadn't been an asshole when Avril had first arrived in Silver Lake to check on Ava, she might be happier to see him. But she wasn't demanding that we leave, so that was a good sign.

"You two going somewhere?"

"Why are you here?" Venus asked in a flat tone.

I tilted my head, struggling not to let my gaze drift down to the cleavage peeking over her tank top. I deserved an award for not staring at her long golden legs. Venus was nearly as tall as me. She was muscular, giving her curves in all the right places. I suspected half the reason she got a hard time in Jade Hills was because her height and direct stare intimidated people.

But I wasn't just anybody.

I liked knowing she could toss me over her shoulder and dump me in a ditch if I was too much for her. I liked knowing that if I treated her incorrectly, she could crush me between her powerful thighs. And what others were too dense to realize was that her direct stare showed me everything she was thinking. She was an open book, but not everyone took the time to learn the language the book was written.

"You know why I'm here." My gaze flickered to Avril. How had she described what was going on?

Venus noticed my unspoken question. "I told her about us. I told her that my family expects me to be married before my birthday and that you offered yourself up as a sacrificial lamb. I also told her I'm not some pathetic lioness that needs a male to take over the hunting."

She'd rather die with her pride. Why? I could see her point. I knew the age difference would be more of an issue than it was for me, but to give up everything rather than give me a chance? I wanted to understand.

For the last ten years, jealousy had eaten away at me, nearly affecting how I felt about Deacon. Even as a fifteen-year-old kid, my ideal mate had been Venus. Not a female *like* Venus. I had wanted *her*.

"Lionesses are the hunters of their pride. The male's role is more to defend their territory."

She rolled her eyes and stomped around me. "I've been out of school too long to tolerate more lectures. We all know how smart you are, Penn."

Her vitriol caught me off guard. I spun to follow her, but Avril pushed around me. "Venus and I have plans. Sorry you drove all this way and we're just leaving."

As if I was going to leave the city without her. "We'll be here for a while."

Avril frowned, caught between wanting to rush after Venus and her curiosity about what I said. "How long?" Her gaze jumped between me and Steel.

"As long as it takes," I answered.

Both girls stared at us.

"Aren't you some fancy professor?" Avril asked. "Don't you have to teach?"

Since I hadn't told anyone, I worked around the truth. "I taught my classes online. Our area's too rural for a university. And I wasn't a professor, I was an adjunct instructor."

Venus's eyes narrowed. Shit. I used past tense. She was too cunning not to have caught that. I had talked to Steel on the way here. He'd said "fuck them" and that was it, but not much seemed to bother him. Except for Avril.

"Well, don't wait around." Venus sauntered to her car, giving me a spectacular view of an ass I could sink my teeth into.

And I would one day—because I was waiting around until she at least talked to me.

FOUR

enus

"So we've done the picnic thing. What now?" Avril kicked her legs out on the blanket.

We had spread our picnic supplies out over the fabric and chatted while we ate. We were in a manicured city park, so the bugs were minimal. It was peaceful as hell, but my mind was not quiet.

My thoughts mulled over Penn. Why had he driven eight hours to Minneapolis to find me? Did he really plan to stay for "as long as it takes"? How could he look so damn good?

Not only that, he must've left soon after he'd learned I was gone. He was supposed to meet with Lachlan yesterday to talk about the contract, yet he'd been here to greet me like the goddamn sunrise.

And then he'd corrected me about the lioness topic. I

had only meant to make a comparison, to make a point. But he had to show off how smart he was, like always.

I should've pointed that out as a reason I was turning him down. What would it be like to be with the know-it-all for the rest of my life? What would it be like to go home to him every day and have him understand what I did down to the chemical and biological level better than I could ever understand?

I could hear him now. *"You know, the color of the dye penetrates the cuticle and blah, blah, blah. And when you curl hair, the heat affects the bonds..."*

No, thank you.

Although learning all of that in his voice would've made my schooling go much easier—

"Venus?"

Startled, I realized I hadn't answered Avril's question. "Yeah, the picnic was great."

"And you studiously avoided the topic of a certain someone."

"To be fair, so did you."

She sat up and crossed her legs. "Ian didn't show up on my doorstep. Ian certainly doesn't have a hot brother."

Yes, Steel was attractive, but he wasn't any of my concern. "I don't want to ruin our day together talking about Penn."

"You wouldn't be here if it wasn't for him. Last night, I purged my soul of Ian. Maybe you need to do that with Penn. Talk it out."

"It's not that." I couldn't purge Penn. If he had done something other than be impossibly smart and sexy, possibly. But he had the nerve to seem like a decent guy. He could get anyone he wanted. There'd be a line if he announced he was ready to mate.

"Why not talk about it and find out what it is then?"

I scowled at Avril, but she was right. It didn't mean I wanted to let my insecurities pour out like messy verbal vomit. "I just have questions more than anything." And a whole lot of baggage.

"Okay. What's the biggest, most looming question about Penn?"

"He was supposed to negotiate the contract with my brother. You know, the old school arranged marriage stuff? So what is Penn going to get for marrying me?"

Avril wrinkled her nose. "What are *you* going to get by marrying Penn?"

My life. "Our families can be a bit archaic. We're very old-fashioned in some ways, and it's seen as Penn doing me a favor." I mumbled the last part, "Since I'm so much older and all."

"That's right, he's how much younger than you?"

I hated answering that question. "Ten years."

"That's not bad." When I rolled my gaze toward her, she continued. "In five years, he'll be thirty and you'll be forty. When he's sixty, you'll be seventy. It's not that bad of an age gap. Look at you. It's not as if you're going to wrinkle and your boobs are going to sag down to your knees by the time you're forty-two and he's growing as hot as his brother."

"Which brother?"

Avril waved it off, but she couldn't stop the blush that told me she wasn't talking about Deacon. "Is your biggest hang-up with Penn seriously the age?"

I let out a gusty breath and collapsed onto my back. I stared at the blue sky as I answered. "Did you know he finished his four-year degree in two years and then he finished grad school by the time he was twenty-four?"

"Ava said he was really smart. Is he really a professor?"

"I have no idea. There weren't many colleges that were going to accept me. I barely passed cosmetology school."

"But you're so good at what you do."

"Yeah, once I'm shown what I need to do, I can do it. I can't take tests and stuff." Grateful I had my sunglasses on, I squeezed my eyes shut. Humiliating.

"There are a lot of people like you. It's nothing to be ashamed of."

"There's not a lot of people like me in Jade Hills. And in Silver Lake, it'd be worse. He's their golden boy."

"Then live somewhere else?"

This was where I would need a human-friendly description. Dragon shifters couldn't live far from their clan, and I wasn't just any Jade clan shifter. I was a child of the ruling family. My place was Jade Hills—unless I mated Penn. Then my place would be Silver Lake, like the previous contract had stated.

Ava was in Silver Lake. I didn't know if my clientele would be willing to travel. I liked the town—no. It didn't matter how much I liked anything. It mattered how much they liked me, and the Jade castoff taking one of the two single Silver brothers wouldn't go over well.

"I need to be near my family," I finally said. "It's one of those things."

Avril started packing up our picnic.

I sat up. "What are you doing?"

"You have questions. He has answers. I think he's the one you need to talk to."

I watched her do all the work, helpless to aid her in getting me back to Penn faster than I wanted to.

She put the last sandwich container in her blue tote bag. "Venus, I know we haven't known each other for long, but you're not a runner. When you heard about Ava, you went right to Deacon to find out what was going on. You told me you have to stay around the family that's marrying you off, so you haven't run from them yet. Maybe you thought you'd give yourself this once, but Penn found you. So face him."

She made it sound so easy. Talking to Penn was the hardest thing to do in the world. When he was the starry-eyed kid who looked at me like I was Venus, the goddess of love and peace, it was amusing. Then he'd gone to college and proven how intelligent he was. And people made comments about how lucky I was that Deacon wasn't like his brother. That I would bring back the nickname used for us—Envy. Because I'd wish I could be as smart as my mate.

A matured Penn, with his charm and his skyrocketing sex appeal? Facing him hurt. But telling him in no uncertain terms would I agree to be his mate was the same as admitting out loud that I would die in just over three weeks.

∼

PENN

STEEL GRUMBLED about his ass for the hundredth time as he adjusted his sitting position on Avril's front stoop.

We had found an Airbnb room about a mile away. It wasn't the cheapest place we could've gone, but it was private and close to Avril's.

"She got to be really a pest, didn't she?" I had said the same thing right after Venus and Avril had left. Did I think the answer would change? Venus had gone from stunned to enraged within minutes, and it had to do with me.

Steel's answer then had been, "Ya think?"

His response this time was a grunt. I was replaying the conversation in my head one more time when he said, "She doesn't like to be told she's wrong. You know that."

I knew it. But it didn't fit the situation. Before when I talked, she'd get irritated. Her reaction today was more personal. She wasn't just annoyed; she was hurt. I draped my arms over my knees. The concrete steps were fucking brutal on the glutes.

"I made her upset over lions?"

Steel snorted and shifted until he got frustrated and stood. "You're a smart guy, Penn. But sometimes you're really fucking stupid."

"Care to enlighten me, wise old man?"

He pointed at me. "You're going to have to watch that shit around her. She's obviously sensitive about the age thing."

I snapped my mouth shut. He was right. Deacon and Steel were each several years older than me. We'd grown up giving each other a hard time about it. But we were siblings. Not the female I wanted to spend my life with.

His expression turned incredulous. "Haven't you paid attention to everything that's been said about Venus over the years?"

I paid attention to Venus. I couldn't care less what anyone had to say about her. Once I got my first boner over a female, I had barely been coherent around Venus. As I matured and gained better control over myself, I could talk to her, or at least talk to others around her. Then, as an adult, she'd been promised to Deacon. I just assumed everyone talked shit because they were either jealous she got to mate him or that he got to mate her.

"I don't care what people say."

"Well, others do. And what they said about her used to be vicious."

No one would guess it, but Steel was the observant one of us. He seemed more volatile, a little unpredictable, but when he acted or reacted, it was after he observed what was going on and made the most well-informed decision possible.

I combed through my brain for what I'd heard over the years. "Her parents were assholes. People aren't sure if her brothers are just as bad or if they intend to do better—"

"It has nothing to do with her family. There was this one time in high school, I went with Deacon to some sort of science meet."

"The Science Olympics." I had been to every one from middle school until I graduated.

Steel pointed at me again. "That right there. Remember that. Anyway, Venus was sitting on the Jade Hills panel. I didn't even know why they entered her; I think someone was just being a dick."

I scowled. Why wouldn't Venus be able to go to the Science Olympics?

"One question had to do with the planets in the solar system. One guy, a Jade Hills kid, made the comment that it was lucky Venus's parents named her what they did so she could name at least one planet in the solar system."

"Bastard."

"So going back to your helpful information, can you

imagine that for the entirety of Venus's life? I've heard similar comments over the years. We're all fucking adults, and they haven't quit. Maybe they go behind her back now that Lachlan is in charge, but people have been trained to act smarter than her. Then you go plug in all those useless facts and to her it's probably just another jackass trying to prove how stupid she is."

I jumped to my feet and got into Steel's face. "Never fucking call her stupid again."

He didn't react. His voice was calm when he said, "Maybe react like that instead of reciting the lion's role on the Serengeti."

Lions have been pushed to the edge of the Serengeti because of human—Oh. I saw it now. I grunted and glowered at the sidewalk. Sharing information gave me joy. It was why I went into teaching. I meant nothing negative by it, that was just the way I was.

And it had gotten me fired. Was it going to cost me Venus?

To her, that was how others ridiculed her. They weren't exchanging information for entertainment. They used it to hurt her.

A car stopped in front of Avril's place. It wasn't Venus's little red Mercury. Did Avril have another friend visiting?

A guy got out. Human. He walked like the muscles of his limbs didn't know whether to propel him forward or fight each other. This human spent a lot of time in the gym.

The closer he got, the stronger a chemical smell grew. It was subtle, not something a human would notice. Our shifter senses were more acute and when someone poured so many supplements down their throat, they started to smell like the plastic casing of the many capsules they took.

"Who the fuck are you?" He stopped at the end of the sidewalk, facing the path from him to the door where Steel and I stood.

"Do you live here?" Steel asked, his voice low, menacing.

I fought to keep from giving him a side-eye. Why so hostile? The dude was rude as fuck, but this wasn't our place.

"I asked first." The man didn't get any closer, but he spread his fingers and curled them into fists.

I knew nothing about Avril's life. This could be her brother. A friend. But his proprietary stance suggested a lover of some sort. Did Avril have a boyfriend? She hadn't talked much about a guy when she had stayed with Deacon and Ava.

The red Mercury pulled into the driveway. The man glared at the car and when Avril scrambled out, he inhaled sharply. Disapproval oozed from him.

"You move on already, Avril? Like I meant nothing?"

"Ian." Avril's startled tone was also full of dismay. She hadn't been expecting this man.

"Who the hell are these guys? You fucking around already?"

A low growl resonated from Steel. He took a step, but Venus stormed toward Ian, making Steel stop. All we could do was watch the show.

She shoved her finger in his face. "Look, Ian. You can't come and go as you please. You can't decide you want to play hide the cock with other women and then come back here when those women don't want to deal with your bullshit. And if you came back here because you forgot your toothbrush or some other nonsense, because let's be serious you're really just more about keeping your options open than doing what's right by Avril and leaving her the hell alone, then you best not be coming up in here talking to her like that."

Ian's face screwed up. He didn't like women talking down to him. "Who the hell are you?"

"I'm the friend that's going to continue to tell her she can do better and help her realize all the crap she had to put up with when she was with you. And since you walked out, what, seventy-two hours ago, may I ask who the hell are you?"

"This is ridiculous." Ian's face had flushed a deeper red the longer Venus had talked. "I came here to fucking talk to Avril, but I can see she's moved on like we never meant anything. Because she's like her mom."

Another growl reverberated from Steel. I put a hand on his shoulder. Venus could get away with what she was doing. To Ian, she was a woman. I didn't know the guy, but I could tell he'd never call the authorities on anything Venus did to him. It'd be a different story with Steel.

Venus closed the distance between her and Ian. "You're going to apologize."

"The fuck I am. I don't need to waste any more time on you or that dumbass."

Venus moved so fast it was hard to see what she was doing until she had one arm locked around Ian's neck and the other wrenching his arm behind his back. Nudging him with her knee up his ass, she made him face Avril.

"Apologize."

Ian grunted, his face beet red. Every time he tried to struggle, she gave his arm a hard twist.

"S-sorry."

Venus hissed in his ear, "You don't sound sincere."

"Sorry! Sorry." He could barely speak while he was in the headlock, but Venus wasn't relaxing her grip. "I forgot my headphones, but you can keep them. Sell 'em or something."

Avril's eyes were as wide as saucers. She nodded, then looked at Venus and nodded again.

But Venus didn't release him. She maneuvered him to his car and stuffed him inside. His tires squealed as he tore away.

She brushed her hands off and sniffed at her shirt. Her face twisted like she smelled something awful. "I smell like a high school locker room now."

Avril's chuckle cut into a sob before dissolving into laughter. "Oh my god, what was that?"

Venus crossed to Avril. "That was me feeling less awful about dropping by with little notice."

Avril put her hand on her chest and caught her breath. "I'm so glad you are here. I'm so glad you came last night to help me see that the breakup was the best thing that could happen to me. And I'm so glad you were with me to make sure he'll never come back." They shared a smile, then Avril's gaze landed on us. "But what are you two doing here again?"

CHAPTER
FIVE

enus

FOR A FEW BLISSFUL MINUTES, I had forgotten that Penn and Steel were in town. My temporary position as Avril's bouncer had been a refreshing distraction.

Penn's gaze was on me when he spoke. I wasn't looking directly at him, but when his attention was on me, it was like the sun shone only for me. "I'd like to talk to Venus in private. It doesn't have to be now, but maybe tonight?"

Of course he'd asked politely, making it hard to turn him down.

Avril waited for me to answer.

"Do you have anything going on today?" I asked.

"I have to get groceries. I could do that while you two talked."

"I'll go with," Steel said.

Before I could come up with an excuse that sounded better than now was too soon, Avril said, "Uh, sure."

Steel gestured to the pickup parked on the other side of the street. "Hop in."

And that fast, I found myself alone with Penn.

"What do you want to talk about?" As if I didn't know.

He approached me. I was still standing on the sidewalk by the garage. "Can we go inside?"

"Out here is fine." Avril had given me the code to her door, but I didn't want to be in a cozy living room with a gorgeous male right now.

His eyes darkened. They were no longer ocean blue. More like lake blue on a windy day. "Can you answer honestly? What is it about me that turns you off?"

I choked on a laugh. Turned off? I had the opposite problem with him. Everything about him turned me on. Until he opened his mouth, or I thought about his age. But he wanted honesty.

"Do you know how it looks for me that you offered to take Deacon's place in the contract?"

He shook his head. "Because of my age?"

"That's a major factor, I won't lie. The kid brother takes the sister whose family didn't want her in the first place."

"I'm not mating your family," Penn said.

"You asked for honesty, Penn. We grew up twenty-five miles and ten years apart. Your parents were decent people."

"Those don't sound like reasons for you not to give me a chance."

"I bet your parents were proud of you." I didn't continue until he nodded. "Mine hated me. I don't know

45

if I had a strike against me because I wasn't a boy, but once I was in school and everyone could witness how stupid I was, then they made sure to let me know they hated me."

"I've heard enough rumors about your parents to know what you're saying. Was it really that bad, V?"

"It was miserable. Do you know how messed up it is that I didn't know how to feel when I was told that their house went up in flames with them in it?" My throat grew thick, and I swallowed hard. "To stand at their burial ceremony and not feel one ounce of grief?"

I didn't mean to tear up. A hot drop rolled down my cheek. Penn brushed it away with his thumb. When did he get so close?

Had we ever stood this close before? His eyes were darker than before. More like denim blue now. He was a few inches taller than me. My brothers were tall, but I didn't spend a lot of time around anyone. Ava and Avril were both average height for females. Otherwise, I spent my days looking down at my clients in the styling chair.

He was *a lot* up close. I could put one hand on each shoulder and see for myself how wide they were. I could trail my fingers down his chest and over his abs. Was he a wall of muscle or was there a secret soft spot to be found?

His proximity crowded out all the bad memories of my parents. He didn't stare at me like he thought my brains weren't worth his time. The way he was looking at me was like I had been walking around my whole life in a costume that others had put on me and, for once, I was bare. For once, someone saw who I really was.

"Penn..."

He brushed his thumb across my lower lip and dipped his head down. When his lips touched mine, I was frozen.

That quickly, I had found his soft spot. Soft, but firm. He increased the pressure until I did what I had considered doing earlier. I put my hands on his shoulders.

A groan left me, only to be swallowed by him as he deepened the kiss. I barely registered the hard flesh under my hands when his hot tongue swept into my mouth.

It was sinful for a male to taste so good. There was a hint of mint, like he had chewed breath fresheners all the way from Silver Lake to a simple suburb north of Minneapolis.

I wrapped my arms around his neck and hugged him closer. I wanted more of the way he made me feel. More of the exquisite pleasure from our connection. More of my body pressed to his, but with less clothing.

Just as the reason we couldn't strip down right now sank in, a faint buzzing reached my ears.

What the hell was I doing?

I jerked away. His lust-filled gaze was sluggish to change to confusion. "What's wrong?"

"We can't—" More buzzing. "Your phone's ringing."

He scowled but didn't go for his phone.

I pointed to his pocket, ignoring the large bulge in front of his pants. "You should answer it."

His eyes narrowed as if to tell me he knew exactly what I was doing, but he finally answered the damn phone.

"Hello?" he said without looking at who the caller was.

I carefully screened my calls. Even my clients knew just to leave messages. My brothers were just as bad. Talking to Ava and Avril was new.

Deacon's voice filtered out of the phone. I'd probably be able to tell it was him without shifter hearing.

"Since you're so close, can you go talk to them?" he said.

"I'm here for another reason," Penn insisted.

"I know, Penn. I hate to ask, but I need both you and Steel on this if I can't be there myself. Ava's just settling in and—you know what, we'll come down."

Penn rolled his eyes to the sky. "No, I'll talk to Steel. You take care of your mate." His gaze flicked to mine. "And I'll take care of mine."

Nerves rippled through my belly, leaving a delicious trail of promise. Nope. I was too used to being disappointed.

"Send me the details." Penn hung up the phone and stuffed it back into his pocket.

I ignored what we had been doing before Deacon called. "Garnet clan up to their old shenanigans?"

"Since your brother mellowed out Jade clan, I swear Garnet wants to take their place."

His phone pinged, and he jerked it out of his pocket to read the screen. "Forty-two-year-old male that a family has been hiding." His mouth tightened briefly. "He's gone feral, but his family chained him and are unwilling to deal with him."

The only way to deal with a feral shifter in our world was to kill him. It was the hardest thing a family could do, but the most merciful. And if they refused to take care of it, then the clan's leader was expected to. All parties must be ignoring the situation if news had made it to Deacon. He must be worried about imminent danger to ask Steel and Penn. In his adult history, I had never heard of him sloughing the termination duty off on his brothers.

My parents had gleefully carried out that particular

duty. "That was probably the only good quality my parents had. Most of us just hoped they took the time to actually prove someone was feral first."

"My father used to say that it was more important to your parents to do it before a Silver did."

"If we didn't have our pride, then we didn't have anything." That should've been our family motto.

Penn's expression turned contemplative. "Is that why you're trying so hard to get away from me?"

"Penn, I just... Yeah. I protected myself for a long time."

"I'm here, V. We have some time. Why don't we just see where this goes?"

I gave him a sad smile. "Because in the end, I know you're just contractually bound."

I would always doubt how he really felt, and as everyone asked themselves why he was with me, I'd wonder too. He didn't seem like a power-hungry male, but he would be one step closer to ruling a clan with me. If something happened to Lachlan, I was next in line and I hoped my brother lived forever.

His dark brows drew together. "There is no contract. Just my promise to you."

Promises to our kind meant life. But Penn didn't have to worry about breaking his promise. If I died first, he'd be free of the constraints of his word.

Wait. "What do you mean, no contract?"

"When I was at Jade Hills, I told your brother I didn't need a contract. I wanted this union to be between you and me and no one else."

"And he bought that?"

"It's the truth," Penn said simply. "And I told him you and I decided we would get away for a while. So, according to everyone else, we're taking a pre-honeymoon."

He was trying to protect my reputation even as I was rejecting him? "Why, Penn?"

"Because you're mine."

～

PENN

THE TALK with Venus yesterday had been informative. Especially the kiss. The kiss had packed a whole storage unit full of information.

Venus's baggage was her parents and her clan. She might have a hang-up about my age, but I was confident that was a minor, and convenient, excuse compared to how she was treated growing up.

A young Venus had built a giant protective shell around herself. There was an invisible exoskeleton encasing her long curvy body.

I didn't want to break it. She'd worked hard on protecting herself. In an ideal world, I would love for her to never need it again. But until that was the case, all I needed was to find an opening and worm my way inside with her.

Steel waited at the door of our rental. "You ready?"

No. I hated clan business. I had spent my entire life thankful that I was third in line for the seat at the head of Silver clan's table. Deacon didn't just oversee our own clan, but all the other clans as well.

"How far away is it?"

I had persuaded Venus to go out with me. A simple

meal to talk. She had barely agreed, but she had relented and we had plans. I had her phone number programmed into my phone and I was antsy to get back to her.

"Two hours."

"Garnet River isn't that far away."

Steel lifted a shoulder. "Pretty close. This family lives in the boondocks. I think when we meet them, we're going to be surprised only one of them is feral."

I could grumble more, but then I would be acting immature and I wasn't going to do that within a hundred-mile radius of Venus.

"Fine."

Steel drove, and I navigated. We didn't have any weapons. We were shifters; we dealt with our problems with force. Intrinsic strength was our only weapon. Guns and knives were tools we hunted with to blend with the humans since it was too risky to get caught with our dragon jaws wrapped around a deer carcass.

The farther north we got, the more trees crowded the road. The highway wound through the landscape until Steel took the exit for Garnet River.

I had never been here. I heard our father describe his trip once. He said they were more compliant than Jade Hills, but something was always off.

The town was small, like most of our clan locations. Older, run-down houses lined the sidewalks. The yards were mostly well cared for, but every few houses was an overgrown lawn full of weeds and decrepit lawn furniture. It was a beautiful day. I expected people to be working in their yards, but the way they stopped and stared as we drove through made the hair on the back of my neck stand up.

"Creepy," Steel said. He offered a wave here and there, but no one returned it.

"You think they know what we're here for?"

"I have no doubt. At first, I thought one of Peridot clan reported them. They're nosy fuckers, but now I wouldn't be surprised if one Garnet called it in. But father was right. The vibe is weird."

"I feel like we're being watched from the shadows." As a community, Garnet River didn't give the impression that they were into self-improvement. It was like the entire community unanimously agreed to let everything die off—the houses, the land, and eventually, the people.

In the past, Jade clan was guilty of using and abusing others to get what they wanted, but they at least tried to help themselves. The same couldn't be said for Garnet River.

The tension in my body uncoiled as Steel drove out of town, but that didn't last long. The more turns he made, the more rugged the roads were. Soon we were bumping along a shoddy path that could barely be called a road.

We arrived at a house well past its glory days. Half the siding was peeled off, several windows were boarded up, and the amount of junk and garbage littering the surrounding land was astonishing.

"Shit," Steel breathed.

The inside of the pickup filled with an ominous air. I wanted to be done with this job, but we were only beginning.

Steel parked by the front of the house, murmuring as he unbuckled his seat belt. "I would've rather parked half a mile away and come up on them in full shift."

"Agreed." But we were stuck doing this like human law enforcement.

Outside, I expected to smell fresh air. But the lawn had been ignored for years. There would be no fresh-cut grass scent. And if the trees gave off a woodsy, earthy smell, the stench of a dank basement smothered it.

Steel let out a cough and I adjusted my breathing to be as shallow as possible. Dank basement was the best smell out of all the smells surrounding us. The most overwhelming was the sickly sweet odor of sewage. I didn't know what these people used for a bathroom, but I wouldn't be surprised to find an open cesspool.

I followed Steel to the door, scanning the trees around us. There were no sounds of people moving around inside or outside the house. The muscles on my back tightened but I couldn't spot anyone watching us.

A surprisingly sturdy new door hung in the door frame. Had they needed to replace this, or was this the beginning of their impossible home updates?

My brother pounded on the door. I glanced at all the windows, half turned to the right, and casually looked around. Then I adjusted my stance, swept my gaze over the windows again, and half turned to the left, attempting to look like a casual observer.

My skin prickled like I was being watched.

My intuition went from a low simmer of dread to screaming in my mind. I opened my mouth to tell Steel something was wrong when a loud blast shook the trees.

A force hit me from behind. I stumbled into Steel, expecting to get taken down by someone. No one was around.

Another shot rang out just as agony blazed through my torso.

"Shit!" Steel crouched, his gaze oscillating between me and the trees. "Penn, fuck. Penn? You've been hit."

Hit? Searing pain burned through my body.

I had been shot.

Another blast echoed through the yard. Steel grunted and dropped to his knees. "We're open fucking game," he wheezed. "Who the hell is using guns against us?"

Someone who thought we wouldn't survive to carry out the proper punishment.

I moved my mouth, but only moans and grunts came out. The pressure in my chest stole my ability to speak.

Another blast. There was a solid thump in my leg, followed by mind-numbing pain.

We've got to get out of here. But the words stayed in my head. Steel slumped on top of me just as I passed out.

CHAPTER
SIX

enus

I PACED AVRIL'S HOUSE, worrying a fingernail between my teeth. I didn't chew my nails, but I couldn't shake a sense of wrongness.

Penn stood me up. I had woken at dawn, and as much as I told myself to be chill about going out with him today, I blew out my hair and gave it a light wave. I had shaved—everywhere. I wasn't expecting to shed one stitch of clothing, but I liked the feeling of being smooth. It was empowering.

I touched up my emerald manicure, painting the ring finger on each hand a shiny silver.

If I wasn't careful, I was going to fall so hard and so fast for Penn that no one could pick me up.

This morning, Avril and I had gone for a walk. I

helped her clean house, even though she insisted I didn't have to. Then she left for work. And I waited.

Penn didn't show. And he hadn't called.

I sat on the couch in Avril's living room, dejected.

I stared at my phone, then set it on the cushion next to me. I snatched it up again. Should I call him? I didn't know him, but this seemed unlike something he would do.

I found his name and dialed. After several rings, it went to a custom voice mail system. As his deep voice filtered into my ear, my anxiety grew.

Was everything all right? Had he changed his mind?

I had lain awake last night thinking about what he said. There was no contract to mate me.

There had been a contract regarding who I was going to mate and what it would mean for both clans since I was a toddler. The final contract had been drawn up when I was in school once my parents realized how much I struggled. Then they figured they'd better tie things up before anyone realized how worthless I was.

Penn's voice mail beeped, and I disconnected. I wasn't on my deathbed, and therefore I would not be leaving a stood-up date message.

He hadn't called. He hadn't communicated. What was going on?

I couldn't worry Avril, so I called Ava. "What's going on with Penn?"

"Oh, okay... you aren't upset with me for telling Deacon that you were at Avril's?"

"It would be shitty of me to expect you to keep secrets from your mate. About Penn?" I couldn't hold back my impatience. "He was supposed to pick me up for dinner. I can't believe he'd drive all the way here and then stand me up."

"Right. I don't know what's going on. Maybe Deacon does." Fabric rustled over the phone like she was on the move. "Deacon? What's Penn up to?"

"Why?" he asked in the background.

I answered before Ava had to relay his question. Deacon would hear well enough. "He arranged to meet me today, and he hasn't shown, and he isn't answering his phone."

When Deacon spoke next, it was directly into the phone. "Tell me everything."

A ball of dread formed in my stomach. I couldn't even be relieved. Something was wrong. I could tell by Deacon's tone. "We talked yesterday, and I agreed to meet with him today. Like a date, but not a date," I rushed to add. "So that was two hours ago and I haven't heard from him."

"Shit. *Shit.* I asked him and Steel to carry out a job for me." His voice grew distant. He must've pulled the phone away from his mouth to talk to Ava. "I've got to hit the road. I have to get to Garnet River."

"If he's in trouble now," I said. "An eight-hour trip isn't going to help him. What was the job?"

"Venus—"

"I'm all you've got here, Deacon. Your brothers have fallen off the radar. Both of them."

The magnitude of how much trouble they must be in crashed into me like a dump truck full of bricks.

"A lot can happen in the eight hours it'll take you to get here." If only we could shift and fly in broad daylight, but we could barely fly at night in the middle of nowhere without being seen. "Let me look into it."

"I can't, Venus. This is Silver clan business. And if shit has gone south, then I need to make sure Silver cleans it the hell up."

"It's my business now. Tell me where he's at or I'll charge Garnet River and rip it apart until I find him myself."

There was a beat of silence. "Here're the directions."

I didn't have to write a thing down. I committed his directions to memory.

"Be careful. It would devastate us if something happened to you."

I couldn't respond immediately. It was the first time someone told me they would miss me when I was gone. Was that why Penn's attention was so disconcerting? I wasn't used to someone wanting to be around me. If they did, they had ulterior motives, like getting closer to my parents or achieving bragging rights about fucking me. My parents were gone, and Penn could get anybody he wanted to sleep with him. And now his family said they cared about me.

"I'll be careful. Just remember, I grew up with Lachlan and Ronan. No mercy."

"Whatever happens, Ava and I have got your back."

I hung up and erased all sentimentality from my mind. I needed perfect calm for this. I sent a message to Avril, telling her I had some errands to run for my brothers. The lie was necessary, and I hated it.

I left her place, got in my car, and hit the road. I pushed the speed limit as much as possible. After scrutinizing every map I could pull up on my phone and GPS, I decided on a route that went around Garnet River. The current leader of Garnet clan hadn't interacted with the rest of the clans much. My parents had sneered over their previous rulers and that told me they must've been decent. The current shifter in charge was young and inexperienced, and all I could think was that it was a good thing my parents had been gone before the young female had taken over. My parents would've seen her as an invitation to mess with her and her clan.

Didn't mean there was any trust there. It was possible they were responsible for whatever was going on with Penn and Steel.

I took all the back roads until GPS said I was about two miles from the house. I slowed until I found a place where I could pull over and conceal my cherry-red car in the trees. It wasn't ideal, but it was the best I could do.

I got out of the car and waited. As impatient as I was, this was critical. From here on out, I couldn't rush. Letting my muscles relax, I let the sounds and smells flow over me. I didn't detect any non-animal movement. No shifter scents lingered on the breeze. I undressed, tossing my clothes and my shoes in my car.

I walked deeper into the trees, picking through the underbrush and avoiding old branches and fallen limbs until I was far enough away from the road.

Then I shifted.

The change took me over as I released the hold on the beast inside of me. She came awake and filled me, stretching my skin, elongating my bones, and adding meat and muscle until I was a full-sized dragon.

We weren't separate entities. She was me and I was her. Instead of green nail polish, I had green scales with a lighter jade sheen overlaying them. The smells of the forest magnified. I could sift through specifics. A jackrabbit was ten yards to my left. A wildlife trail that deer preferred was a hundred feet to the right. The only shifter scent I detected were dragon shifters, but their scent was off. I couldn't identify it. It was like someone had gone for a month without bathing or brushing their teeth, then they took a shower and one cleanup wasn't enough to remove the grime of an entire month. That was what their smell was like, except the shifter themselves were dirty. Like they had been tainted down to their very souls and couldn't be washed clean again.

I started my two-mile trek through the trees. Moving my big body through densely populated woods wasn't easy. I had to take it slow, and I would stop frequently to listen.

Before I could see the house, the smell of blood assaulted my nose. My heart hammered against my ribs. Penn was injured. Steel too.

I ran through the information Deacon gave me. Four adults. Two parents, and two children. If the male was forty-two, was there another sibling close to the same age? Our kind relied on the stability of a mate. If the other sibling was single and over thirty-five, it was possible they were also deteriorating.

It was unfair, but it was our nature.

I edged closer and closer to the house until I could finally see it. The acrid scent of gunpowder reached me.

Guns?

Guns weren't an oddity among shifters. But we didn't use guns as weapons. They were a tool to procure food.

I sniffed again. Gunpowder and blood. Had someone shot Penn and his brother? That was illegal in the human world, but it was instant death in the shifter world.

I couldn't charge the house and rip it to splinters looking for the guys. What was the opposite of what my parents would do?

Risking the extra time, I circled the house. Trees crowded the unkempt backyard. Overgrowth and bushes provided enough concealment. I detected another shifter's scent, but it was faint and smothered by the awful smells coming from the yard and house. Perhaps the anonymous informant?

I shifted back to my human form, my bones and skin shrinking into the smaller package I was more accustomed to. The shift wasn't painful, nor was it pleasurable. It was no different than walking or doing push-ups, it just required more exertion.

Nudity didn't bother our kind as much as humans, but anxiety threaded through me at the thought of being naked around this unknown family.

I'd have to make sure I didn't get caught.

Going back to the days when my brothers and I were kids, I darted through the yard, hiding behind whatever I could get to in a quick burst. Just like when Lachlan played hide-and-seek. The first one found had to battle his dragon. Neither Ronan or I wanted to be found first.

Finally, I reached the house. The window above the bush I was hiding by was boarded, but I couldn't get that close to the house without scraping myself raw from the branches. The old farmhouse had cellar doors on the side with a giant padlock hooked around the handles of the two doors. Nothing on this property looked as new as that chain and padlock.

The scent of the brothers grew stronger and my nose latched on to the familiar sandalwood, cedar, and coriander smell. Penn was close. I scanned the area around the cellar. Blood dotted the ground.

I had a decision to make. Without knowing if they were down there for sure, who was with them, or how many people were in the cellar, any plan I came up with seemed risky.

I could pick the lock and sneak down, though it was hard enough to sneak up on a shifter in close quarters. Or I could shift and break my way in. I didn't smell any humans on the property, but I didn't want to risk it.

I waited a couple more minutes. A snarl and a yell resonated from the cellar.

Fuck it. I shifted as I walked. The opening was barely large enough to fit my dragon through, but I'd make it work. I gripped the chain and the padlock in my claws and ripped. Both doors wrenched off before the metal gave. I tossed them to the side and dove headfirst down the wooden stairs.

My vision adjusted quickly, a byproduct of the centuries my kind spent living in caves. The same type of chain that had been on the doors was wrapped around both guys and a knife handle protruded from each of their abdomens. If they couldn't reach the knife to withdraw it, the wound couldn't heal. They must be in agony. Across from me was an iron cage. Inside, a male prowled in his dirty, bony human form. He ignored me as if I was nothing. Every few steps, he lifted his nose into the air and snapped. The action was followed by snarling and growling. The cage was too small to shift, but the male had lost all sense of humanity.

Oh my god. Steel and Penn were going to be this male's lunch. This was the feral that had been reported to Deacon.

Penn pried his eyes open, and his face screwed up when his bleary gaze landed on me.

I took a step toward the guys when Penn's eyes widened. I sensed the movement behind me and whipped around, the bony armor at the end of my tail crashing into the cage. The old, rickety structure rattled like nothing was holding it together but Elmer's glue. The door to the cage squeaked open.

Frustration poured through my veins until I roared, a deafening sound that boomed through the small space. I'd been told my whole life I wasn't cut out to be the leader of Jade Hills, that it was a good thing Lachlan was born first. I had been raised to believe that none of this work was for me. Yet here I was. And I was supposed to be on a date.

In a dark corner, a female not much older than me with hair and skin as greasy and dirty as the rest of the property was wedged between empty shelving units. She snarled and gnashed her teeth, as far gone as the male I assumed was her brother. There was no cognition in her gaze, and her actions were wild and erratic.

I had to do what no one else had the courage or ability to before now.

My dragon arms weren't long enough to yank her from the corner. One of my shoulders caught on a railing and my wing knocked in to the dim light hanging from the ceiling, but that didn't stop me from stretching my neck as far as possible and snapping at her.

Instead of backing farther into the corner, she launched herself at me. She screamed, and maybe she would've tried to shift, cramming both of us into the basement with our sheer dragon size, but she didn't have time. Her scream cut off when I snapped my jaws around her neck.

Just as she went limp, the feral male threw himself onto my back. His slight weight shouldn't have slowed me down, but he was getting heavier.

Was he shifting?

The thought of him shifting on my back sent panic through all my muscles. There was no room to fight, and we could hurt Penn and Steel. I thrashed and bucked.

The male's claws were embedded in my sides. I whipped around, but the move was sluggish. The two of us could barely fit in the cellar, and with him as a dragon on top of me, we filled the space between the floor and the ceiling. If I shifted back to my human form, his teeth would do what I had done to the female.

So I launched myself toward the cellar door. The move ground his head into the ceiling and his grip loosened. I tried another leap. He was knocked off, and his claws disengaged from my sides. With him off my back, I crouched low and spun around, holding my tail tight to my body.

The dragon I faced was sick. He was skin and bones, and half his scales were missing. His eyes were empty; nothing but a beating heart and primal urges drove the body. When I locked my teeth around his neck, he gave up the fight. It was as if I was the unanswered prayer he had been waiting for.

As his life drained out of him, his form shifted back to human. I lowered the body to the floor before I let it go.

The beating of my heart thundered in my ears. The places he had bitten and clawed me burned. But I would heal.

I took one last look at the two dead shifters and listened for others. Not hearing anything, I lumbered toward the guys, shifting as I went.

Steel was still passed out, but he was alive. Penn watched me. I jerked the knife out of Steel's belly and tossed it to the side. Then I did the same for Penn.

"When you stand a girl up, you do it in style."

~

PENN

I TRIED to keep from groaning while I was sprawled out in the bed of Steel's pickup. Venus had trashed the stairs in the cellar, but between her dragon and what strength I had left, we got the both of us and Steel out of the cellar. She searched the house and found the parents dead in the bedroom. Without them, the adult kids had been left with basic survival urges.

I would never forget what I saw. Two hopeless and helpless shifters. A magnificent Venus. And a glimmer of hope in a desolate environment.

She had come after me. Instead of assuming the worst of me, she'd assumed the worst of the situation and she'd been right.

The sun was setting. I stared at the darkening sky. Two stars were bright enough to shine through the fading light and a sliver of moon was off to the right.

Venus had driven Steel's pickup to where she had parked her car. Fresh air surrounded us instead of death and decay. Deacon would talk with the council to make sure the family was properly buried by the clan that had failed them.

Steel and I had spent the rest of the afternoon and evening in the woods, lying in the back of his pickup, trying to heal enough to move on our own.

Venus had called Avril. She told her friend that Steel and I had gone for a long hike and had slipped off the trail, hurting ourselves. For a fabricated story, it wasn't the worst. But it wouldn't explain a few rifle wounds or a stab wound, but it bought us time.

Venus had said she was going to get us back to our Airbnb and stay the night to make sure there were no complications while we recovered. Avril had wanted to help, but Venus assured her we wouldn't be leaving the bed, and Avril had to work the next day.

I cranked my head on the hard pickup bed to inspect my brother. He'd taken two rounds to the torso and was worse off than me.

He didn't open his eyes. "Will you quit staring at me and just ask me if I'm okay?"

Relief poured through me. If he was that cranky, he was getting back to normal. "I like watching you sleep."

He finally cracked an eye open. "You were always the weird one."

I chuckled, then winced. "Ow."

Venus leaned over the side of the pickup. "Oh, good. You're both waking up."

Steel's eyes were closed again. "I wish I was still asleep. Zero out of ten, do not recommend visiting Garnet River."

My chuckle turned into a cough. "Ow, dammit. Quit making me laugh."

I was tempted to close my eyes and snatch a little more rest, but I couldn't take my gaze off her. Her hair was tousled around her head, dried blood ringed her neck and matted her hair, but she was like my own personal angel. Her dragon was gorgeous. Sleek and strong, with a jade tone glossing over her scales.

I wanted her more than ever, but I could barely lift a finger right now.

"I took a quick look around that place. Putting together everything with what I saw, the parents had kept their son locked up because he had gone feral, and they didn't want to put him down. But their daughter was going the same direction too. She had just turned forty. So with the parents gone, she tried taking care of the brother, but she could barely take care of herself. When you two were called in, I assume she thought she could get two birds with one stone. Bigger game for her and her brother to feast on and get the Silvers out of the way."

"She had to know that wouldn't work. Even if Steel and I had become breakfast, lunch, and dinner, others would follow when we disappeared."

"Ferals aren't known to think clearly, but I know what you mean. Something doesn't seem right."

As much as I wanted to keep staring at her soft features, I let my eyelids drift shut. "I don't know people as well as I know textbooks."

"People are complicated, but at the core, they're very simple."

"Maybe if I had your skill with them, I wouldn't get catty reviews from my students."

"Smarty-pants Penn Silver gets bad reviews?"

I opened my eyes to shoot her a glare. "About me teaching, V. I get rave reviews everywhere else."

A faint blush stained her cheeks. "What do they say? I can't imagine anyone complaining that you're their teacher."

I couldn't move away from Silver Lake, and that benefited my work. As a twenty-five-year-old college instructor, I wasn't much older than ninety percent of the students. The separation online protected me from breaking any fraternization policies, not that I had wanted to.

"The first semester I taught, one student wrote 'it's a good thing he looks pretty, otherwise I couldn't keep my eyes open while he droned on.'"

"Ouch."

"My personal favorite is 'thank you Mr. Silver for proving that looks aren't everything.'"

Venus broke into laughter. She had to step away and double over. When she draped herself over the side of the pickup, she was grinning. "I'm sorry. I shouldn't be laughing."

"No. It's okay to be humbled sometimes. It's good for the ego."

Her smile faded. "As long as it's not all the time, I suppose it doesn't hurt."

"I got fired." I had been planning to tell her when we went out tonight. We weren't at a nice meal, and I didn't have her to myself. But she should know that I was a jobless mate prospect when she ran her own business and had been doing so since I was in middle school.

"Why would you get fired?"

As I'd suspected, she wasn't surprised. She'd caught my slip earlier.

"Long-windedness, poor student experience, and an inflexibility in regard to adjusting to other teaching methods."

"That sucks, Penn. I'm sorry."

I grunted. I'd told her, and that was all I wanted to dwell on for now. "You going to be our nurse tonight?" Shifters healed fast. We hadn't been immortal for eons, but we'd been able to keep our healing abilities. Still, there were limits, and Steel and I had been close.

"I can give you a nice trim and a good foot soak. I don't know about the nurse part."

"You already saved our lives."

She averted her gaze like what I said embarrassed her. "Yeah, but I had to take two lives." She gave her head a shake. "I don't know how my parents were so cavalier about it. I know Lachlan doesn't enjoy it, but now I'm wondering if I should check on him."

My female had a heart as large as her personality. "I'm sure he'd appreciate it even if he didn't say anything." When Deacon had to carry out a termination task, Steel and I met up with him to grill and shoot the breeze. He wouldn't forget what he'd done, but he'd know he wasn't alone.

As peaceful as it was in the middle of the woods, this wasn't where I wanted to be. I wanted to get my brother and Venus out of Garnet clan territory. With a groan, I rolled to my side without disturbing Steel and sat up. Venus rushed around to the tailgate to help me as I scooted to the edge. With my legs hanging over, I caught my breath. My lungs burned, but I could breathe easier than I had been able to for hours.

I patted Steel's leg. "Think you can tolerate getting into the back seat?"

A long groan left my brother. "If it gets us out of this godforsaken territory, the suffering will be worth it."

We were of the same mind. I eased to my feet. The world swayed, and I gripped the edges of the tailgate.

Venus put her hands on my shoulders to steady me, inspecting my features. I wish I could brush away the worry in hers.

"Are you going to be all right?" she asked.

I stole a few moments to get lost in her green eyes.

"Just a little dizzy. It'll pass as I heal. The dizziness is probably due to blood loss. I'll be anemic for longer than it took my wounds to heal. Eating foods high in iron like red meat and—"

She kicked up a brow.

"Oh, I'm doing it again."

She patted my shoulder.

I released the tailgate and put my hands on her waist. If I wasn't so bloody and filthy, I'd try to kiss her again. "I'm sorry I missed our date."

"It was only lunch." She might have convinced herself it wasn't really a date, but I knew it was.

"Thanks for covering for us with Avril."

"Deacon will probably beat us to your place."

"Good thing we rented a house with two bathrooms." The corner of my mouth kicked up. "But we might have to replace all the bloodstained towels we're going to create."

Behind me, Steel shifted his legs. "We're going to end up camping out here all night if you two don't hurry."

I ignored my brother. "As soon as I'm healed, I'd like a redo."

"As long as you promise not to get shot again."

"The damage from high-powered rifle rounds depends on the type of bullet, the path the bullet followed, and its speed," I groaned. "There I go again."

She cocked her head as she peered at me. "You don't know you're doing it?"

I shook my head, risking an increased pounding against my temples. "I like learning. I forget that not everyone else does."

She dropped her gaze and quietly said, "I like learning too."

"I'm full of random knowledge. I'm happy to share, and if you've heard it before, you can tell me to shut up."

"I have a feeling your brothers tell you that enough."

"I'm certainly thinking of saying it right now," Steel said as he tried rolling to his side.

Venus and I rushed to help him, but I couldn't shake my goofy grin.

CHAPTER
SEVEN

enus

THE NEXT MORNING, I opened the door of the Airbnb house to a fraught Ava and a grim Deacon.

She flung herself around me. "I was so worried. I'm so glad you're okay."

My throat grew tight. Lachlan never asked for my assistance when he carried out feral terminations, but our parents had dragged me and my brothers to enough when I was younger. And they'd had an *only the strong survive* mentality. No one had worried about me.

I hugged her back. "It was sad more than anything." My kind was used to the reality of being single after a certain age. We didn't dwell on how fucked up it was that we had to bind ourselves to another in order to keep the fabric of our being from dismantling. But I'd thought about it all night. That family had been dedicated to each other. Why couldn't that be enough?

Why couldn't I be blissfully alone in my little house in Jade Hills and enjoy my time with my clients? Yes, the silence after work weighed heavy on my psyche some days. I wished I had someone to talk to. I enjoyed hearing the playful laughter of the kids next door. But no relationship was better than one that'd bring back the hard times from my younger years.

Ava pulled away. "It had to be awful for you."

I stepped aside for them to enter. I had slept in Penn's bedroom. He refused to let me sleep on the couch. Steel hadn't been able to argue about giving up his bed. Penn and I had dragged him to his room to collapse on the bed. We'd have to replace all the bedding in addition to the towels.

So I'd stayed in a bed that Penn had slept in before. His unique scent had tucked me in and if it weren't for my need to recover from my own injuries, the smell of him on my skin would've kept me up.

I'd showered before I went to bed and again when I'd woken. His scent was still all over me—and I had a hard time minding.

I led Ava and Deacon into the house. Penn was sprawled on the couch. His bare chest was visible above his blankets. He'd showered last night too.

When he opened his eyes, his deep-blue gaze was on me, not his brother.

My belly flipped and my body warmed like I had just shifted and puffed fire all over myself. I didn't have this reaction around males. I was usually suspicious of their intentions. I had been wary of Penn's intentions. I was still, wasn't I?

He was jobless. That didn't explain why he wanted to take his brother's place and mate me. I had a tidy hoard of jewels and I made a decent living with my work, but I was hardly flinging bills around town.

I needed a distraction. "I'm going to check on Steel. He lost a lot more blood than Penn." I gave Penn a playful look. "He needs lots of iron-rich foods."

Humor glinted in his eyes. He lifted his chin to Deacon. "Go ahead."

Deacon followed me into Steel's bedroom. A metallic tang hung in the air.

Steel rolled from his side to his back and blinked at us. "Shit. How long have I been out?"

"It's only the morning," Deacon answered. "Venus wouldn't give me the address, so you guys could rest."

The sheen of respect in Steel's eyes wasn't what I normally got from other shifters. Today definitely wasn't what I was used to. "I can run and buy some new bedding. We'll trash this stuff if you want to shower and bag all the dirty linen."

Steel grunted to a sitting position, palpating the healed spots on his chest. Scars remained. Two sizable pucker marks that would eventually fade completely. "Fuck, that hurt."

"I'll go with Venus," Ava said from behind me. "You guys deal with Garnet."

It was easy to forget this wasn't over for the brothers. The situation shouldn't have gotten out of control. There were things clans could do. A mating bond was all that was needed. The couple didn't need to have a close relationship, they just needed to play the game of shifter-kind.

In the living room, Penn was folding the blankets he'd

used. Bronzed muscles rippled along his back. He wore nothing but basketball shorts.

He glanced over his shoulder, pinning me with his blue stare. "I put some money on the coffee table. And before you reject it because you have plenty of your own, it's a write-off. Deacon's here on business. We ruined the bedding on his official business. Let Silver clan take the hit."

His explanation brought more relief than irritation. I could've covered it. Why was I worried if I planned to stay single past my birthday? And Penn wasn't in it because of my money or he wouldn't have made his clan absorb the cost.

Nothing was clear anymore.

"Thanks," I mumbled and located the cash on the coffee table he'd pushed against the wall the previous night to keep out of his way.

I couldn't breathe easier until I was in my car and there was no shirtless Penn to be seen.

"How are you really doing?" Ava asked after she got in.

"Confused," I answered honestly.

She frowned. "About last night—oh. Penn?"

"I'm learning he's a nicer guy than I thought." And an excellent kisser. "But that doesn't change the issue."

"What exactly is the issue?"

Why couldn't anyone else see the problem? It was like I was making it up, but why would I do that?

If her tone had been less concerned, invested in me as a person, I wouldn't have talked to her. I had clients, and I was friendly with them, but they weren't friends. I listened to them talk and helped them work through their problems. My relationship with my clients was one sided.

Ava and Avril were my first experiences at a real friendship. They hadn't grown up under my parents, didn't fear me because of them, and weren't shifters. When we'd met, I had been a blank slate. And they'd treated me in a way Venus Jade had never been treated before.

I told her my concerns with a guy like Penn, the youngest and smartest Silver brother. And in my opinion, the most handsome. Ava probably wouldn't agree on that part.

When I was done, she laid her warm hand on my arm. "I'm not going to nag you about mating him. I don't want to lose you when I've only just found you, but it's your life and your decision. So I'm just going to give you something to think about. You've lived your entire life bombarded by others' words and opinions. What if you can have a life without all that garbage weighing you down?"

I frowned. "That's what I have. I don't want to lose it."

"Is that what you have? Or have you figured out how to hide yourself in front of everyone? Have you limited what you can do because you're too scared of it happening again?"

No. I wasn't hiding. I lived in the same town. I ran a business.

"You're not a kid anymore, Venus. And your parents are gone. Just think about it."

"Okay." I had already thought about it. "Thanks for not nagging. It doesn't make it easier when everyone thinks I should thank my lucky stars anyone wants me while also ridiculing me for who it is."

"Have people been awful?"

I opened my mouth to say yes, but I couldn't summon any instances. "Not much has happened yet. But it's coming."

Her dubious look didn't help convince me I was right.

～

PENN

"I CAN'T LET this go. I'll have to address it with Garnet clan." Deacon paced from wall to wall in the living room.

Steel and I sat around the dining room table. I could raze through all the shifters of Garnet clan. Yesterday had cost me a date with Venus.

At the same time, a quick chat in the back of the pickup bed had broken down a part of the wall she had built between her and everyone else. Now it felt like there was a section open just for me.

"When are we going to confront their ruler?" Steel asked. He had bags under his eyes, but he'd rally at Deacon's word.

Deacon's gaze brushed over our brother. It was a miracle Steel was still alive. Sheer stubbornness and adrenaline had kept him from bleeding out. The stab wound hadn't helped, but after being shot, it was more like a nuisance. Like being pinched while being beaten with brass knuckles.

"First thing tomorrow. I need you two at full strength."

"Then I'm taking Venus on a date tonight." My brothers were staring at me. "What? I'm not risking standing her up again."

"I think she understands you didn't stand her up," Deacon said.

"Doesn't matter," I replied. "I almost bled out in the basement when I could've been with her."

"You've got it bad," Steel said as he laid his head back and closed his eyes. "Worse than I thought."

"It was a good thing we were here," I said, ignoring him. Yes, I had it bad. I'd been like that for a long time. "Or Deacon would've walked into that by himself."

Deacon shook his head and propped his hands on his hips. "I probably would've. I would've traveled here alone to keep from bothering either of you." He gestured at Steel. "You're our only police force in Silver Lake." He waved at me. "And you have your own job to handle."

"About that. I got fired." I'd told three people. It still felt like shit, but I was accepting reality better.

"What? Why?"

"I'm a shitty teacher."

"Kids don't like lectures these days." His tone was resigned, otherwise I'd be offended.

"Bingo. Anyway, something like this could happen again." I rose and started pacing the room like Deacon, only my path was meandering instead of straight back and forth. "Our kind wants to modernize with the times, but sometimes it's getting harder to tell where our humanity ends and the dragon begins. Humans are getting married later in life, or they're not getting married at all. Shifters see that and wonder why they can't have that too. If they haven't met someone they want to spend their life with, then why do they still have to sign a part of themselves away to keep their sanity? We're going to see the limits get pushed to dangerous levels."

"It's the way of our people," Deacon said.

Not only was his point valid, it was the only point he could make. When our kind traded in mortality for human lifespans, we also traded our way of life. Our natural aggression couldn't be denied. We needed an outlet, whether it was fighting or fucking or, I didn't know, extreme chess? We needed a mate to hold us accountable, to share the burden of the emotions that we dealt with and humans didn't. A human mate could do that. Because they knew. And that was the pinnacle of what we needed, someone who knew if we were taking care of ourselves and could inform authorities before someone got hurt.

I had already found that person. I could have ten years left of single life, but I didn't want to spend one more day without Venus.

And after yesterday, after seeing what happened when we defied our natural laws, I could see why Venus was willing to risk execution to keep that from happening. And after talking to her, I understood why she preferred execution over settling for any mate who would take her.

I wasn't just any mate. I had a few weeks to get through to her. Garnet clan was being a pain in the ass, but I wouldn't let them get in my way.

I said what Deacon was most likely thinking. "Are you wondering how many more shifters like that Garnet is hiding?"

He nodded, his expression grim. "They're growing more and more unstable. With Lachlan's rise to ruler in

Jade clan, Garnet has deteriorated. And it doesn't make sense."

"Civilization is encroaching on them. We're not any different than other animals when it comes to that. We go against her own nature when humans start eating up our home and our natural order. Garnet might've settled in northern Minnesota generations ago, but the large population of central Minnesota, of where we're at right now, is closing in."

My mind started ticking through the stories of animals running wild through neighborhoods. Moose kicking over garbage cans and ramming cars. Coyotes hunting dogs and cats. Mountain lions stalking hikers on trails. Those weren't shifters. Those were animals trying to survive in an ever-increasing human population.

"We're part animal, and Garnet is responding with their animalistic side, shifter style."

Steel watched me, his eyes blurry. "Leave it to the scholar to figure out what's going on at a biological level. But my guess is that we're dealing with clan politics."

Deacon had claimed that my scholastic ability was like a gift as a member of the ruling family. He could share his energy to heal a human. Steel could erase short memories of us from them. And I could learn facts that helped our kind develop.

I couldn't read people, and Steel was probably right. This was a political issue, and I was probably worthless. Venus might've been made to feel stupid her entire life, but when it came to functioning in society, my ability to glean information from textbooks didn't make it easier for me to adjust in social environments.

"I'll have to meet with Garnet," Deacon said. "They

might not have found the bodies, but they had to know the family would draw me here."

"I'll go with," Steel said.

I nodded. "I'm not going anywhere as long as Venus is here. If you need help, I can help. As long as it doesn't interfere with my date tonight."

Steel scratched his head. "Was I out cold when he asked her on another date?"

"No, I haven't asked her yet."

The corner of Deacon's mouth kicked up. "You are persistent, I'll give you that."

The front door opened, and Ava and Venus spilled in. Plastic bags rustled, and they were talking over their plan of attack for cleaning all remnants of blood out of the house.

Venus glanced at the three of us, but her gaze landed on me, stroking over my bare chest and following my abs down to my waistband.

When she caught me watching her, my grin widened. "Tell me where you need me to start cleaning."

"You're recuperating," Ava said. "You need to rest."

I shook my head, holding Venus's gaze. "Nope. I'm going to help clean so we get it done. Because I'd like to take you out tonight."

Venus clutched her bags tighter. It might've been my sudden request or all of our witnesses, but she stammered out an "okay."

My smile didn't waver. "Okay?"

"Okay." She finally broke her gaze away and looked down at herself. I didn't know what she saw, but I saw a powerful female with a body I wanted to get lost in for the rest of my life. "I need to go back to Avril's and get cleaned up."

Ava glanced at Deacon. "I'll join you. I don't want Avril to find out that I'm in town without telling her. But we need to decide on the story."

Deacon and Steel started coming up with the plan, but I crossed to Venus and took the bags from her hands.

"So, what do you like to eat when you're not rescuing males from ferals?"

CHAPTER
EIGHT

enus

I HAD NEVER BEEN in this position before. Avril and Ava waited outside the bathroom door.

"I can't wait to see it!" Ava's voice trembled with excitement.

Shivers traced over my body. I was full of anticipation too. I gave my reflection one last look. My hair was blown out, and I put enough curls in to give my blonde locks some dimension. The green ends brushed over my chest. I wasn't wearing anything fancy, but I had picked up a new pair of baby-pink shorts to go with a white camisole top. I looked like a life-size Barbie. The effect wasn't that much different from how I normally looked, but that I put in this level of effort was unusual.

I opened the bathroom door and faced my new

friends. "It looks like I'm trying too hard. It looks like I'm trying to look younger."

The last part bothered me. My looks had never been my issue. For them to top my worry list when I needed to be the most cognizant was unsettling. I needed to stay strong to keep from succumbing to Penn's charm.

Part of the problem was that I didn't want to resist him as much as I used to. Talking to him while he was recovering in the back of the pickup made me see him as a real person, and not the ideal male that many others would kill for. He had flaws. He wasn't perfect. And that made him more appealing.

"You look like Venus," Avril said. "You always look gorgeous, so I think it would be really hard for you to look like you're trying too hard."

I brushed all my hair over one shoulder. "You're right. Everyone knows it's my brains and not my looks that make me incompatible with Penn."

Avril gave my arm a squeeze. "It's the people who think you and Penn are incompatible that are the ones with the problem."

"I guess the last problem to solve is which shoes should I wear?"

I mostly just wanted to move on from the topic. My choice was jewel-encrusted flip-flops, but if one of them insisted on my wraparound sandals, I would go with it just to make it look like I had really needed help to decide.

The shoes I wanted to wear were their pick too. Just as I was slipping them on, the doorbell rang.

"I'll get it," Avril said as she rushed for the stairs to the landing.

Deacon and Steel were coming here with Penn. Deacon and Ava had gotten a hotel room. Avril had bought the story about the hiking mishap, and that Deacon and Ava had to come check on them.

Penn's voice filtered down the stairs as he addressed Avril's concerns about how he was feeling. "I heal fast. No need to worry about me."

Steel grumbled, "I heal fast too."

"Then you need to quit being so clumsy." Penn laughed.

I could picture Steel's scowl, especially around Avril. I wasn't sure if the others noticed his increased moodiness around her, but I had enough going on. I would stay out of it.

"If you remember, I was helping you," came Steel's reply.

I rushed up the stairs.

"I remember perfect—" Penn's mouth hung open as he stared at me. His hot gaze traveled down my body, stopping at my mint-painted toenails before leisurely working his way back up. "You look great," he said in a reverent tone.

"Thanks. You do too." As if I had to tell him. He always looked good. But he wasn't in his normal jeans and a T-shirt. He wore a navy-blue polo that made the blue of his eyes as pale as the winter sky and pants that hugged his legs and tapered to stylish shoes.

I hadn't seen one male in Jade Hills dress like that. His look was youthful and trendy. Was I too casual?

Deacon pushed through the door behind his brothers and beelined straight for Ava, as if the two hours they spent apart had been excruciating.

Penn caught my bemused expression and rolled his eyes. "Ready to go?"

"Sure." I almost ran back down the stairs and into my

bedroom. What was I doing? Did I think I could resist Penn? Did I think that my mind and body would react logically around him?

But he was holding the door open for me and my legs moved of their own accord.

Outside, he rested a hand on my lower back as he guided me toward his brother's pickup. "I found a hibachi grill not far away."

When he had asked me what I liked to eat, I had said I just liked food. Ava and Avril had asked enough pointed questions to get out of me I had always wanted to eat at a hibachi grill. Only I hadn't known the name. My description had been "one of those places where they prepare the food in front of you and there are flames and they flip their cooking utensils around."

Of course, Penn had come up with the word for what I was talking about.

He opened the door for me. I climbed in the passenger side and tried not to ogle as he walked around the front of the pickup to climb in.

Once we were closed in together, his sandalwood, cedar, and coriander scent curled around me. I inhaled deeply without being obvious. Did I smell as good as him?

I was determined to go into tonight with an open mind. What Ava said had gotten through to me. What if I was letting everyone else decide what was too good for me when none of them had taken the time to get to know me?

Penn turned on his GPS and maneuvered through traffic until we were parked in front of a restaurant a few miles from Avril's place.

The savory smell of cooked meat and seasoned vegetables assaulted my nose. "That smells divine."

"I'm sure it tastes better."

In the restaurant, the seating was what I would've wanted yesterday. Side by side and among too many other people to have an intimate conversation. We were put with ten other strangers to surround three sides of the grill. The chef preparing our meal was entertaining, and the food was even more delicious. But by the time we were done, I was ready to have Penn to myself.

He paid for the meal and seemed content to stay as long as I wanted to. But as the meal had gone on, the seating arrangement no longer worked for me. "Is there somewhere we can go to talk?"

"Do you want dessert?"

I always wanted dessert. I liked to garden, and I ate more vegetables than many other shifters I knew, but I had a raging sweet tooth unlike many others I met.

Desire must've been scrawled all over my features. Penn grinned. "Let's go look for a fun dessert place."

He took my hand, sliding his strong, warm fingers against my palm. His grip was firm and confident. My knees were rubbery as we walked out of the place.

This male was potent.

When we were back in the pickup, he pulled up nearby dessert shops on his phone.

"Do you feel like ice cream, cake, macarons, crepes, or cookies?"

"Yes."

He chuckled and glanced up. Then realized I was serious. "All right then. We'll stop at the first one we find and work our way through them."

Before he threw the pickup in reverse, I said, "You

don't have to do this. I know you're a hardcore meat eater." He'd ignored his rice and vegetables at dinner, and he'd ordered two extra servings of steak.

"I like a treat."

Not like I did.

When I didn't respond, he put the pickup in park and twisted in his seat, resting his hand on my headrest.

"Venus, watching you get pleasure will never be too much for me. I don't care if it's when your eyelids flutter over a small morsel of zucchini cooked on the hibachi grill or a gallon of cookies and cream ice cream, I'm all in."

Heat flushed my body, coiling between my thighs until a pulsing started that was difficult to ignore. As much as I wanted to eat all the things he listed, the last thing I wanted to do was endure more polite conversation in public when I really wanted him all to myself.

But also—ice cream.

"Why don't we get that gallon and go back to your place to talk?"

∾

PENN

WHEN MY CRUSH first started on Venus as a teenager, I wouldn't have believed anybody if they told me I would have her all to myself on the couch with a bowl of ice cream. But here we were.

I knew more about Venus than I did before dinner, and that had been one of my goals. She loved desserts, and while she might discriminate about who she'd go on a date with, she had very few restrictions for sugar-rich food.

We picked up scoops of ice cream from a novelty ice cream shop. There were also two more pints in the freezer. She had chosen a cake batter flavor as her base for her pint and the cup of ice cream we came home with. I picked mint, a flavor I shouldn't be able to go wrong with on the date.

She had kicked off her fancy sandals and stretched her legs onto the coffee table. I could barely taste my ice cream. There was too much golden flesh in front of me I'd rather feast on.

I had only finished half of my treat. I placed the cup on the coffee table before I gave myself an upset stomach. It wasn't as bad as getting shot twice, but it could ruin the night.

"Aren't you going to finish that?"

"Be my guest."

She paused midscrape of the bottom of her cup. "You have to be sure. Because I'll decimate it."

My dessert was watching her inhibition with goodies. I tried to recall the time I had seen her so content, so interested in what she was doing. She wasn't on guard. It was like the sugar drugged her, weakening the wall she had built until I finally got a glimpse of the real Venus Jade.

"I'd love nothing more than to watch you devour my ice cream."

She rolled her eyes, but a smile played along her full lips. "All males are the same, I swear."

"The only reason that would offend me is because I don't think you've been treated very well by those other males."

The wall was back in place. I only hoped that the portion of it we had chiseled away was still gone.

She snatched my ice cream and didn't bother to trade out spoons. I liked seeing her pink lips close over a utensil my mouth had just been around.

God, I had it bad.

"No, I wasn't treated very well. But it could've been worse."

I wouldn't tolerate the way she justified crap behavior. She was a decent person. I had never heard of her being intentionally cruel. People liked to talk about how harsh she could be, mean even, but few considered the entire situation. In every instance, Venus had been standing up for herself or someone else. Mostly, she defended herself. No one else would.

But I had to tread carefully. "I'm sure being part of the Jade family kept some of the worst treatment at bay, but it also invited a lot more."

She shrugged and stuffed another spoonful of creamy goodness in her mouth as if she wanted to prevent having to talk.

"You didn't deserve it. Better or worse than what others have experienced, you didn't deserve it."

"Felt like I did," she mumbled. She polished off the rest of the ice cream, and I waited, sensing she was going to say more. My patience was rewarded. "I didn't do well at school. Awful really. It was embarrassing. For me, for my family."

"How was school hard?" I noticed the telltale sign of her shoulders tightening. Shit, I needed to clarify. "I'm not denying that it was hard for you. We all have different abilities, but I doubt Jade Hills teachers were encouraged to troubleshoot what was actually going on. Most of the time, it's an issue of learning style, not intelligence. And honestly, even if it was a matter of IQ, it doesn't justify shitty treatment. There are ways to teach everyone at all levels."

She stared at me, working over what I said. I worried I went too far, pushed too hard, but it was a topic I was passionate about. I loved learning. I enjoyed school. And I didn't understand why no one else was as thrilled as me with surprise quizzes.

Learning was my passion. That was why I felt like a giant failure as a teacher. Had I made a miserable learning environment for the students in my classroom?

She straightened as if she committed to explaining no matter what I'd say. "If I hear the information, I understand it. If I see someone do a procedure, I can replicate it. I always did better in labs, but then it would come to the quiz and I would struggle. And there was all the other bullshit. No one wanted to partner with me. Teasing. Bullying." She shrugged and shoved her empty container into her other one. "And it was like the teachers loved telling my parents all about my struggles."

Something about what she said clicked in my brain, but I didn't address it yet. "Why would they love that?"

She gazed at her lap where she was absentmindedly polishing a nail with the fingertip of her other hand. "Some teachers had my parents as students. My dad struggled in school too. Lachlan and Ronan weren't the best students, but they didn't have as hard a time as me."

So she learned better in an auditory format, and there was a family history? "Did you find written work harder because the letters often didn't make sense? Like they would move around or float off the page?"

She met my gaze, disbelief in her eyes. "Yeah?"

"And in math, did you have problems remembering the steps, and did the numbers behave in the same way as letters? The same numbers and letters didn't always look the same?"

She nodded, her eyes round.

"Venus, I think you're dyslexic. And you probably have dyscalculia. It makes sense if your parents struggled. I wouldn't be surprised if one or more of your grandparents did too." It would certainly explain a long line of learned meanness. Generation after generation getting teased and bullied through school when they were supposed to be held up as the top family would fuck anyone up.

"I'm not dyslexic. I'm a shifter."

"Shifter's brains can be wired differently. Just like some are right-handed and others are left-handed. You said you learn better when you hear it, but when someone rattles off a long list, do you get the steps confused?"

Her jaw clenched. "I can keep track of stuff."

"I'm not saying you can't. I'm just saying your brain processes information differently. They say it's a learning disorder, but I disagree."

"Why?"

"Because twenty percent of the population is dyslexic. If one out of every five people learns in a specific way, then why is that considered a disorder? The main problem is that our school systems don't teach reading, writing, and math in a way that one-fifth of their students can ideally learn it. And they don't do it even when that way is also how all the other students can still learn. It's messed up once you think about it."

She was quiet for several moments. Her green eyes

were troubled. I had meant to make her feel better, to give her some understanding that she wasn't broken. There was nothing wrong with her.

"So if I have kids, they'll be the same?"

"It's possible, but everyone is different. Some people struggle with reading, others struggle with alliteration before they even start reading. I had a friend who could remember a thousand military history dates, but he couldn't say some names correctly two times in a row. Another was a whiz at math, but his handwriting was so illegible he got the nickname Doc. He didn't separate his words."

Her eyes shimmered. Tears welled until one rolled over her eyelid to track down her cheek. I surged toward her and caught it with the pad of my thumb.

"Venus, I only meant to make you feel better."

"I'm not—I don't—" She made a frustrated sound in her throat. "I don't know what I feel, but I know I don't want to pass my childhood on to the next generation. And it's crazy I'm even worrying about that when I might not see next month."

Meaning she might not make it past her birthday if she doesn't take a mate. "Your kids are going to be just as strong and brilliant as you. They're going to be fighters, and they're going to be compassionate, and that's a trait you're going to put back into the Jade clan." I stayed next to her, soaking up the heat of her body.

"I used to get told I was lucky that I wasn't mating you. That I'd only be jealous of your intelligence and it would embarrass the clan."

"Who said that?" I would kill them.

"Different people over the years. The better you did,

the more comments I heard. Usually older people, my parents' age."

That explained it. Her parents had indoctrinated an entire generation of people to embody the Envy nickname, to covet what others had instead of seeing their own strengths. They had thought it'd conceal perceived weaknesses.

"Fuck them, V. They were wrong, and there's a lot of people who know it."

She turned toward me. "How are you so nice?"

"I'd like to think I would be nice anyway, but I've had a crush on you forever."

A laugh sputtered out of her, and she sniffled. "Stop it. When you were a teenager, I was in my midtwenties."

"Didn't stop you from starring in every one of my fantasies."

"Penn! I didn't look at you that way."

"Oh, I was painfully aware. I realized you were supposed to be my brother's mate, but when he met Ava, and I could see that there would be no one else for him but her, I took my chance. And I won't quit trying to win you over."

"I might've noticed..." She ran her tongue along her lower lip and avoided looking at me. "I've noticed you lately. Since you came home after school. And definitely at the cabin when Ava was there."

I resisted the urge to pump my fist in the air. I paid little attention to winning females over. When I went out, I wasn't interested in a long-term relationship. I wasn't interested in who my future mate would be. It had been Venus when I imagined who I'd end up with. And even though I had known it couldn't be her because of the contract that had been between her and Deacon, a part of me wouldn't quit hoping.

The flame of hope had only grown into an inferno. "What did you notice?"

Her expression went flat. "That you're a lot younger than me."

"But still an adult."

She pressed her lips together like she didn't want to answer. "Yes. I noticed you were a fully grown man, and it was really hard not to have inappropriate thoughts about you."

"They're not inappropriate if I fully support every dirty, sexy fantasy you have."

Pink brushed along her cheeks. "Penn."

I was gaining momentum, and I wouldn't quit now. "Tell me one. Just one naughty thought you had about me."

CHAPTER
NINE

Venus

THERE WAS no way I was considering answering him. How had this night gone from a date I had tried not to call a date to... this, whatever this was? It wasn't like any date I'd been on. I had been enjoying one of my favorite desserts, then I'd been crying on the couch next to him, and now I was failing to stop the flood of raunchy images that had formed in my mind about Penn over the years.

"Just one," he prodded.

The biggest problem was that I wanted to answer him. I wanted to tell him everything I dreamed of him doing to me. This male saw me. He was probably one of the smartest shifters in the world, and I told him how much I had struggled in school and he continued to be undaunted. Not only that, he had explained what was going on with me after only a few minutes of conversation. That was more than any of my teachers had granted me.

Penn made me want to share more with him.

"When you're with your brothers, they're always telling you to quit talking about one subject or another." Oh, god, this was it. I was going to tell him. Just one fantasy, that was all. But it was a doozy. "I thought a guy that talks that much must be amazing with his tongue."

His expression went blank for a millisecond before astonishment took over. But by the next heartbeat heat infused his blue eyes, turning them midnight blue, and they were focused on me.

"I am a fast learner. I'd like to think cunnilingus is something I excel at. Would you like to be the judge?"

I had prepared for embarrassment. I wasn't prepared for the hot press of desire into every cell of my body. Or the automatic spreading of my legs and the way he shifted off the couch until his knees hit the floor and he was wedged between my thighs. I wasn't prepared for the way he snatched one of the sheets he used last night and shoved it under my ass.

But by the time his fingertips curled around the waistband of my shorts and he slowly tugged them down, I was ready in so many ways.

With my shorts and underwear off, I was fully bare to him. His greedy gaze brushed my center. God, I must be dripping. This man had me so turned on I almost couldn't see straight.

"Where do you want me to put my tongue, V?" He slipped a finger through my folds. "Here?"

Brief contact was like a lightning bolt to my groin. I jacked my hips up with a moan, needing and wanting more.

"Or here?" He slid his finger to my entrance and lazily circled around the opening.

I tried rolling my hips to take him deeper, but he continued to tease me. "Yes," I panted.

"Yes, what, V?"

I liked the way he called me V. It made me feel like a different person, like the person I saw reflected back in his eyes. And I wanted to be that female. "Yes, I want your tongue there too."

He slid his finger back up and circled my clit once. "You want my tongue here"—he teased my opening again—"and here?"

"Yes." I sounded like I was begging.

His grin was downright feral when he dipped his head. He swirled his tongue in the same places his finger had been. Back and forth, circle. Back and forth.

The males I had been with didn't leave me with a high standard of what pleasure could be like in bed. I had done more for myself with a couple of toys than anyone else had.

All Penn had used was the tip of his finger and his tongue, and I was nearly out of my mind. Every muscle in my body strained to hold my legs open, to hold still but move with him, to keep from coming in seconds.

I had to tip my head back and stare at the off-white ceiling. The sight of his head with that thick glossy hair between my legs was erotic as hell.

No, I couldn't resist. I had to watch him. I might never get this again. He said he was committed, but a lot of guys had been interested until they had me. I had been nothing but a conquest for them. Penn was younger; the thrill of getting me to succumb to him may be larger.

So I was going to take the pleasure he was willing to give.

He flicked his gaze up to catch mine. His eyes were nearly black, and the way he undulated his tongue was nearly enough to tip me over the edge.

I wouldn't last much longer. I had never gotten off from oral play alone. I usually needed something to ride, whether it was a toy or a finger. But I shattered against Penn's mouth. Wave after wave washed over me, making me buck and ripping his name from my lips. He didn't let up, but went at me harder, tilting his head. I twined my fingers through his hair and held him to me as I rode his face. I might be embarrassed about this later, but right now I didn't care. The sensations were next level. It was like a lightning storm lit up every pleasure center in my body. A million tiny explosions forming one Big Bang.

When I couldn't take it anymore, I collapsed against the couch, releasing his head.

He wiped his face off on the sheet and lifted my shirt to lay a kiss on my belly. He kissed farther up my stomach with a ravenous expression.

"Do you want to tell me one more?"

∼

PENN

THE WAY my pants constrained my erection was one of the most painful things I had ever experienced. I was harder than I had ever been in my life. Anything before Venus suddenly seemed like it had all blended in with my teenage years. The early days when I barely knew what to do or how to do it.

Her scent surrounded me. She was the sweetest fucking treat I'd ever had. I wanted her legs wrapped around my waist while I was driving into her. I wanted to sink into her heat and never come back up for air, to fuck her for hours and hours and hours. Then I'd let her sleep and be right back at it.

She was boneless. She'd come so hard I knew she needed a breather. But this flimsy top hinted at how spectacular her breasts would be. I had to see them. I had to know if her nipples were the same shade as her dusky-pink lips. I wanted to draw one tight peak into my mouth and show her I was pretty damn good with my tongue there too.

"I don't know if I can survive telling you one more." Her hands were back in my hair. She didn't stop me as I gently tugged down the neckline of her shirt to the top of her lacy white bra. "Maybe it should be my turn."

I wasn't relinquishing control.

One last tug and there they were. Round, creamy globes, as full and voluptuous as the rest of her.

Goddamn, I didn't know I was such a tits guy.

The heat cranked up in her gaze, and her arousal sharpened. Her stamina matched mine. I knew it would, but I would adjust myself to whatever she needed.

A grin spread across my face as I finished freeing her breasts. I palmed them, loving the weight in my hands. Her legs were still open, cradling me. If I didn't have my damn pants on, I could shove inside of her and tongue her nipples until I made her come again. Would she count that as two fantasies, or one?

"I've dreamed about these."

She arched into my grip. "You're a boob guy?"

"I'm a your boob guy." Of course I liked breasts, but I had never been as riveted as I was now. "I want to lick and suck your nipples while I'm buried deep inside of you. While my mouth is right here, I want you to come around me." I touched a fingertip to one pebbled peak.

That red tongue of hers flicked out to lick her lips again. Fuck, I wanted that in my mouth too. There was nothing on Venus I didn't want to taste.

"Is that one of your fantasies?"

The corner of my mouth curved up. "This is so much better than anything I could conjure up."

She ran her lower lip between her teeth. "Do it."

I ripped my pants open so fast the button went flying, and I didn't care where the hell it landed. Cool air kissed my shaft.

I positioned myself, her wet heat kissing my shaft—

Voices outside the door made Venus gasp. Alarm shot down my spine and straight into my dick. The effect was nearly painful, but when I shoved myself back in my busted pants, agony seared through my tender flesh.

Venus flew off the couch, yanking her top in place and almost knocking me out with her knee. She found her shorts and jumped into them just as the front door opened.

She stared at me with wide, horrified eyes. I gave up trying to close my slacks and left my shirt hanging over my flagging erection.

"Oh, shit." Steel's stunned tone broke through our panic. "Sorry, fuck. If I knew—"

Venus frantically combed her fingers through her hair and smoothed the long strands over her shoulder. "No, it's fine."

A growl resonated from my chest, and Steel chuckled. "Doesn't sound like he thinks it's okay."

Venus's blush raged over her cheeks.

I rose and made sure everything was covered for both of us. "You could've called."

"I did, but I can see why you didn't answer. Don't worry. Deacon and Ava went back to their hotel. I can get a room too."

"No," Venus said quickly. My pride took a dent. She didn't want to spend the night with me? "I came here to visit Avril. I don't want her to think I would ditch her in a heartbeat to get laid." She gave me an apologetic look. "I treasure her friendship."

Right. I felt like an ass. She didn't want to crap on her friend's hospitality and I couldn't blame her. "Can we plan something for tomorrow night?"

Steel held his hands up. "I'll find somewhere else to be."

"I'll talk to Avril and Ava."

That was the best I was going to get. "Let me change my pants, and I'll take you home."

Before I made it to my bedroom, Steel stopped me. "The Garnet ruler got a hold of Deacon. The council discovered what happened, and they figured Deacon was going to pay them a visit. They requested the one that killed their shifters come along."

"No fucking way."

"It's fine. I can go," Venus said in a bored tone. She rolled her quelling gaze toward me. "Since I'm also from a ruling family and can decide for myself."

I held up my hand. "Sorry. I just don't want you to have to fight anyone else."

"I might not have to. We'll see." She lifted a shoulder.

"But I'll have to talk to my brothers. I'll be there on behalf of Jade clan."

Right. This was about more than Venus. The whole situation involved three clans. It was politics, and my bad luck made it a giant cockblock.

CHAPTER
TEN

enus

I WAITED until Avril went to work before I called Lachlan. I explained the situation, leaving out the date. "So that's what happened, and Garnet's council wants me to go with Deacon and his brothers tomorrow."

"I don't give a fuck what Garnet wants."

Typical Lachlan.

"I don't either. But I'm here, and I'll go. What do you want my stance to be?"

Lachlan blew out a hard breath. "Are you mating the Silver pup?"

Lachlan rarely evaded answering questions. But I couldn't figure out what one had to do with the other. "It doesn't help when you call him a pup."

"Come on, Venus. We all know he's an adult."

"But you're all going to give me shit for his age."

"So? You going to take it?"

This seemed like a lesson reminiscent of our parents. I wasn't in the mood. "I'm going to have to take it from the entire town. For once, I'd like to have my brother's support."

He let out a disbelieving snort. "If you didn't have my support, I would've challenged Deacon for ditching my sister and risking her life less than a month before her birthday. You lived your whole life expecting to have a mate by now, and he changed his mind at the last minute. But you didn't seem to care. In fact, you seemed happier. And don't think Ronan and I haven't noticed how you get when Penn's name is mentioned. So this is me supporting you. By letting you do whatever the fuck you're doing."

I had never known Lachlan to be as logical as he just sounded. He relied on force, not like our parents, but enough to get his point across, enough to maintain his power. "Who are you, and what did you do with my brother?"

"There's a lot you don't know about me." He said it so matter-of-factly that I could only blink and stare at the wall.

"Is everything okay?"

"So what I need you to do," he said as if I wouldn't call him out on ignoring my question and I probably won't. "Is go to Garnet River with the Silvers. I want you to put up with zero shit—we are Jade after all—but I want you to watch everyone. And then tell me the vibe you get, and what the overall feeling is toward our clan."

Lachlan was putting me to work? When our parents dragged us along, they'd made it clear I had no role in the clan other than to mate Deacon and tie us to Silver. But at the heart of my awareness was the fact that I would never have to worry about it.

Lachlan had seemed to humor my presence more than anything. I didn't get the impression he resented my existence like I had with my parents, but asking for my insight in a situation was unexpected.

"Should I be watching for something specific?" I asked.

"Just a general feel. I know our clan hasn't gotten along with most of the others, but Garnet is a little more untrustworthy than most."

"Most of the other clans would've said that about us not too long ago."

He grunted because I was right. "They've been quiet for years. I don't want to be the clan they decide to fuck with for a power play and since you were the one who put the ferals down instead of a Silver brother, they might see their chance. I want to know what you think—of the way they handle the situation, and their general position in our world. I've finally gotten our clan to a point where they're not easily provoked and I don't want Garnet fucking it up. "

My respect for Lachlan grew. There was more going on with him than I thought. I had been satisfied that he wasn't a brutal leader, but if he was proactively protecting the clan, then he was a better person to be in the position than I thought. "I'll tell you everything that goes on."

"The vibe is all I care about. Deacon can deal with the rest. I've got enough on my plate."

"It'll just be my opinion."

"People behave differently around you. They're trying to challenge me or Ronan, but because of the precedence our parents laid for your treatment, they don't monitor themselves around you. They don't kiss your ass, but when they challenge you, it's about a perceived weakness that our mother and father instilled in all their minds. Believe me, I've noticed that very few shifters have ignited a brawl with you since they died. They won't admit our parents were wrong, but they're freer around you. It gives you a unique perspective. You've always been good at reading people, and I'm banking on that ability tomorrow."

He thought I was good at reading people? Maybe Lachlan could extend his healing power to another like Deacon did with Ava's dad, but I'd never known him to try. And I doubted that my parents or my grandparents had physically healed anyone. To them, that would be a sign of weakness. Ronan wouldn't tell us if he could turn water to wine, much less wipe a memory like Steel or solve a calculus equation like Penn. Ruling families were given enough extra abilities to help their clan hide in the human world.

Innate or learned, I knew people, and I could use that trait to help. "I'll call you when we're done and when I have a moment to myself." I wouldn't hide what I was doing from the Silver brothers, but I didn't have to announce it. Besides, Deacon was savvy enough to realize that what transpired would reach my brother.

"That shit's out of the way. What's going on with Penn?"

As much as I wanted to tell him it was none of his business, it absolutely was his business. Lachlan would have the grim task of terminating me. I owed him an update, not an evasive response.

"We're talking."

Last night flashed through my mind. Penn's head between my thighs. It was a good thing I wasn't in the same room as my brother. My reaction would be embarrassing.

"Talking about setting a date or how you want him to fuck off."

"I'm thinking about it."

Something muffled the other side of the phone, but I heard the heavy sigh. "Look, I'm having a hard time not commanding you to mate the kid—guy—whatever. I did that once and—you need to make the decision that's best for you, but dammit, Venus. This isn't fucking easy for me."

Who had he commanded to mate? Indy? Oh my god, that would explain so much. Sympathy flooded my mind, and it was even better he wasn't around to sniff it out.

"I appreciate it, Lachlan. I really do. We went out last night."

"How did it go?" he asked in a half-interested tone.

I couldn't stop the choked sound I made. How was I supposed to answer? I would've had Penn buried deep for as long as possible but his brother walked in?

He snickered. "Gross, but that's what I want to hear."

"Goodbye, Lachlan." I was smiling when I hung up. Because I was actually considering accepting Penn's mating proposal.

~

PENN

· · ·

108

AVA STAYED BEHIND WITH AVRIL. She had made some excuse that Venus and I were accompanying my brothers on some Silver Lake business. Ava spun a fairly believable story about Garnet River being interested in establishing a camping and hiking lodge, and Venus was tagging along since her brother was in charge of parks and recreation in Jade Hills.

The Turtle Mountains had plenty of camping and fishing choices, and while Avril was familiar with the area, the two towns were a little farther north, pushing into the border, she didn't know them as well. Nor had she ever been to Garnet River.

Since Ava wasn't accompanying us, Avril was happy to hang out with her.

Venus rode in the back seat of Deacon's pickup with me. She'd given me a little smile when we picked her up but didn't give me any other sign that she had dwelled on our evening together like I had. My dick was in the various states of erect, depending on whether I was thinking of Venus. I had tried jacking off in the shower. Four times and I had still barely gotten a decent night of sleep.

Deacon drove the familiar route that Steel and I had taken to Garnet River. He turned down Main Street, a run-down stretch little longer than three blocks. There couldn't have been more than six inhabitable buildings. The rest were in various states of demolition, unless its neglect had caused several structures to collapse in on themselves. Demolishing these buildings and cleaning out the lots must've required more resources than Garnet River could spare.

"Is that their city hall?" Venus leaned toward the middle in order to peer out the windshield.

I did the same just to be closer to her. Her sweet white chocolate scent caused a rush of blood back to my groin, but I didn't pull away. I was going to take what I could get.

Next to a giant rubble of brick was an old two-story building. Unlike its neighbor, the place was made of wood and had an old-time saloon look to it.

"It's the only building they seem to have put some effort into," Deacon replied.

Prickles erupted over my body. In unison, we all scanned the surrounding area. We were being watched, and not in the open, like when Steel and I had gone through earlier.

A few beat-up old cars and rusted-out farm trucks lined the street on either side. Across from what we thought was city hall was a narrow diner. Up ahead one block, a gas station with two simple pumps sat alone.

"I almost feel bad for them," Venus murmured. "Jade Hills wasn't the easiest place to grow up, but we were better off than this."

The muscles in Deacon's jaw flexed as his grim gaze took in the dilapidated buildings around us. "The state of Garnet River has been ignored too long. I know I haven't been out here since I took over, but if I had heard reports about how bad it was, I'd like to think that I would've made it a priority."

Steel shook his head. "No wonder it was an anonymous call that phoned in the feral siblings."

Anonymous. I'd like to know the story behind the phone call. Was it meant for Silver to deal with the siblings, or was the ulterior goal to draw us here?

Deacon parked, and we climbed out of the pickup. Deacon's vehicle probably had more value than all the vehicles around us put together. Not probably—most certainly.

The tingles across my shoulders didn't leave. Casually, I looked around, lifting my gaze to the second level. A form jerked away from the window. I hadn't been able to see much detail, but it looked like a female.

"Did anyone else see that?" I said, barely moving my lips.

Deacon responded the same way, speaking only loud enough for us to hear. "Did you see who it was?"

"No."

When we walked into the building, the smell of musty basement surrounded us, fogging out the scents of any individuals inside. We were in a small vestibule facing a wall with an opening on either end leading to a dim hallway.

Steel swiveled his gaze between the two options. "Right or left?"

I smelled the new arrival before I saw him. His scent wasn't unpleasant, but unlike most shifters, he used cologne. Most perfumes and fragrances were too strong for shifters to use, but could hide the stronger scents of emotions—like fear and anxiety.

His weak smile couldn't hide the anxiety in his expression. "Follow me please. We're expecting you." He scurried in the direction he came from without waiting to see if we followed.

Deacon led the way as a show of power while I fell behind the group. Venus didn't hide her open curiosity. As we walked down the narrow hallway, we passed a conglomeration of photos. Everything from the early days of Garnet River to the most recent class photos hung on the wall. None of the pictures had more than fifteen shifters in the graduating class, with the last few years' numbers in single digits.

Was the population dwindling? Did the clan shun human mates? Was inbreeding a problem?

Our kind mated with humans, or Deacon wouldn't have Ava. For centuries, mating outside of our kind functioned as a way to keep our population robust and healthy. The offspring would unfailingly be a shifter, but over the generations would offer variation in our genes.

Garnet River's small population and decreasing amount of kids didn't mean they were inbreeding or refusing human mates, but it could be a sign of another problem. After being in town for so short a time, the only thing I knew about Garnet River was they had problems.

We were led into a large open room that was once the main area of the bar that city hall used to be. Three older shifters sat at a long table at the end of the room. The male who retrieved us joined another male and two females. One female nodded to four chairs in front of the table.

Were we expected to sit in front of their council like a lineup of naughty children?

Deacon didn't sit, and the rest of us took his lead.

"Which one of you is Deacon Silver?" the oldest of the females asked.

"I am," my brother said. He made a deliberate show of looking around the otherwise empty room. "Where is your leader?"

"She was unable to make the appointment."

Shock rippled through the rest of us until I couldn't tell where my emotion ended and my brothers and Venus's began. An incident that injured not only two from the ruling family, but one from Jade's ruling

112

family, and the leader had elsewhere to be? It was unheard of.

"Get her." The command in Deacon's voice was unmistakable. It was an order, and his tone said they had better comply or there would be consequences.

Consternation crossed the face of the oldest female. The council ran the show, and I would bet my house that the other three members of the council had relatively little power compared to their elder.

The female who had spoken folded her hands on the table and smoothed over her features. "You must understand—"

"Get her." Deacon raised his voice. A show of power came next. The council had to know, but they didn't move.

They were playing a losing game of chicken.

Deacon picked up a chair and tossed it to the side of the room. He picked up a second chair and lobbed it. Wood splintered and clattered against the wall and onto the floor. His actions did two things—gave the council a big middle finger for the way they set the meeting up, and proved that he would challenge if need be. He did the same with the third chair. Unease made each of the council members squirm. Three of them looked to the oldest female as if silently pleading for her to do something.

When Deacon reached the fourth chair, he slammed it over his knee. "From the state of this town, I regret ruining your property. But this meeting is costing me time and money, and we're here to talk about an attack on my family. I said get your leader. You'd better go fucking get her or my brothers and I will dismantle this town, starting with the rafters of this building."

Deacon stopped in front of me and Steel. Neither of us moved. Venus didn't shift or twitch. We were a united front.

A soft voice from the back said, "I'm here."

I hadn't seen the shadow in the window very well, but I was convinced she was the one who had been watching us.

Had she been hiding? Or had the council taken power from their own ruler?

The female was younger than me. Long dark curls hung halfway down her back and she wore linen shorts and a solid-colored top like Venus. Her bare feet whispered against the wooden floor. She was a slender female, to the point of being unnaturally thin. I didn't give much thought to a female's body shape, but her appearance concerned me. Shifters didn't get sick. Was she getting enough food?

She stayed at the edge of the room, her gaze studying us. On the outside, she appeared calm and collected, but the knuckles of her folded hands were white and a faint tremor shook her body.

Deacon pointed to the long table. "Take your station in front of the council."

Irritation flashed across her face, but she smoothed it over. She reminded me of my students. Old enough to be independent and hated to be told what to do, yet in no position to defy authority. If she didn't like being told what to do, why was the council acting as if they were in charge?

She took her time walking to where Deacon had pointed, as passive-aggressive a move as any I had seen, and so unlike a ruler.

"What the hell is going on here?" Deacon demanded,

speaking to no one but her. "My brothers and a family friend were attacked—by your people. Two shifters who'd deteriorated so badly you can't convince me you didn't know. Explain yourself."

The female trembled, but she did her best to hide it. "The Trevino family were always reclusive. They weren't hurting anyone. I admit we didn't know the extent of the situation."

"All clans have birth records." Deacon swept his hard gaze over the four members of Garnet's council. "And it is their responsibility to regularly monitor them for mating noncompliance."

She lifted her chin. "One slipped through the cracks."

Steel was the one who replied. "It was not *one* that slipped through the cracks. Both siblings were feral."

Her stoic mask nearly slipped. "We were planning our intervention."

"You just claimed they slipped through the cracks." Deacon cut a hand through the air. "I'm invoking Silver law."

The council grumbled and the female paled, but a beat of relief shone in her dark eyes.

"What's your name?" Deacon asked.

"Brighton."

"Brighton Garnet, your clan will fall under the rule of the Silver clan until I can determine what is going on here and correct it."

Brighton's brows pinched together. "How can you come here and just take over?"

"How can you be so ignorant of the rules of your people?" Deacon's question was hard but not unkind. He genuinely wanted to know.

Brighton crossed her arms like she was hugging herself. Was she even twenty-one yet?

"If you are exerting your control over us, then I assume you're going to protect us from Lachlan Jade's retaliation for what happened to his sister?"

"I will handle Jade."

Venus didn't react. She was probably wondering what a young, frail ruler like this was doing in charge of the clan already. I racked my brain about Garnet clan. My father had mentioned that he was working with the council until the ruler came of age. Something about an accident. I hadn't paid attention, figuring it would be Deacon's problem one day. I'd had my schooling to care about.

The hubris of a young shifter male.

Did Venus recall the story? No aggression was in her stance or her expression. She watched Brighton and studied the council.

The female lifted her chin and her reddish-brown gaze jumped over me and Steel. "May I propose a solution?"

Deacon was wary when he gave a curt nod.

"You have a brother close to my age. I propose a mating contract between the two of us."

"What?" Shock rippled through my system.

Venus made a choking sound in her throat.

"He's promised to someone else," Deacon answered flatly, and I owed him. Brighton wasn't the female I wanted to mate, and I sure as hell didn't want to move to Garnet River.

Brighton's gaze turned shrewd when it landed on Venus. "I understand time is running out, and his meeting proposal has not been officially accepted. Therefore, Penn Silver is free to mate. It would make more sense for him to mate me than a member of Jade clan now that Lachlan Jade has proven to be a more stable ruler than the previous ones."

We all stared, dumbfounded, as this meek, uncertain female assaulted us with clan logic.

CHAPTER
ELEVEN

enus

THIS SLIP of a shifter wasn't trying to steal my male out from under me, was she? But from the way my teeth throbbed to sink into her slender neck and my fingers curled as if my talons were visible, she apparently had done just that.

No, I hadn't accepted Penn's proposal. I hadn't even started considering it until last night. But I'd been prepared to have Penn to myself until my birthday. I'd had time, and I feared it'd just run out.

"Did you set this whole thing up just to meet him?" I had been passively monitoring the situation like my brother had asked. Spectating had gone out the window as soon as Brighton exercised her right to propose a mating deal with Penn.

"I did no such thing." All hint of a tremor was gone

from Brighton's voice, but I inhaled deeply. Was she lying? I couldn't tell, and that was unusual. Lies stunk. "The attack and today's confrontation showed me that our clan has been too long without oversight. We are isolated from other shifters. Our numbers are dwindling, and knowledge is getting lost from generation to generation. Did I know about the feral family? I had some idea. But you've seen the state of Garnet River."

Brighton threw her hands up and gestured around her. I couldn't believe the sudden movement didn't bowl her over. The girl needed a sandwich piled high with as much meat as one slice of bread could hold.

"You're isolated, but somehow you know I didn't throw a giant celebration when Penn offered to replace Deacon? You've told different stories, practically in the same breath. Maybe you need to get your shit together before you try mating yourself off."

"Venus…" Deacon's warning was subtle, but if he didn't put an immediate stop to it, then he wanted to see how far I would take this. He wanted to know how hard he should fight for what his brother wanted.

I wanted him to laugh and tell her it was ridiculous, but that was the issue. Her proposal wasn't ridiculous. Mating Penn would mean that Deacon wouldn't be stretched between Silver Lake and a nearly defunct clan eight hours away in another state.

Deacon had just mated with Ava. They were starting a life together, and he faced leaving her for long periods of time. Not to mention the danger. What if there were more families like the Travinos?

The unselfish thing to do would be passing over Penn so this female could have him.

A tiny voice in my mind asked me about what he

wanted. But I had been raised under the same shifter laws as Penn. We weren't the oldest and sometimes, our mating status was best used for the clan. I had grown up with that knowledge.

Yes, I wanted Penn. I couldn't ignore that after the other night. I wanted the way he made me feel, but I didn't want all the complications that came with him. And now having him might come with a cost.

"Deacon," Penn said in a diplomatic tone. "I request that we take time to gather information before any decisions are made."

I whipped my head to stare at him before I could school my expression. Hurt crowded in my chest, making it hard to breathe. He was considering it?

My lungs were on fire. I sucked in a shallow breath. Had he seen Brighton's willowy, fragile beauty and decided that the opposite of me was actually more up his alley?

The oldest female on the council spoke. "I agree with the youngest Silver. It won't hurt to take some time. Much of the damage has already been done." Her ancient gaze scanned the room, touching on the debris Deacon's outrage left behind. "Perhaps we should move this meeting to another room, where there's more seating."

I barely heard her. Gathering information was Penn's thing, but he claimed to have it bad for me. Yet he wasn't rejecting the female's idea.

And I was back to feeling like the fool. I was the girl who could barely understand what was in front of me while everyone around me was caught up and reading ahead. For once, I thought I had been in charge of my life. I thought I got to use what pride I had and explore a possibility I had previously rejected. Penn had convinced me I could.

Lachlan thought I was good at reading people, but today only pointed out that he'd had good reason not to include me on major clan decisions.

What was I going to tell my brother? I could tell him of my observations, but what if he agreed with the female's request? What if the thought of tying Garnet clan forever to Silver benefited Jade? We wouldn't have to worry about their retaliation regarding my interference with the feral, just like Garnet wouldn't have to be on edge about us. And once I explained how destitute this clan was, he might even agree it was the best thing for dragon shifters to make a nearly dormant clan strong again.

What if Penn mating Brighton was the best thing for our people?

Wasn't that what the contract between Deacon and I had been about? I had been willing to do that for the good of our kind. Was I willing to create more conflict where we could solve several problems?

I was confused. Conflicted about how I felt. Chagrined. I thought I had claim to Penn when I'd been ready to shove him away. And distraught to realize that the age gap between him and Brighton was only a few years. A much more relatable time frame for Penn.

I wanted to storm out. But I hadn't driven myself. And I would look foolish. Weak. I had had enough of that in my younger years. The smartest thing to do right now would be to follow Deacon's lead and show I had more brains than people gave me credit for.

PENN

THE ROOM we were led to was on the upper level, where I'd seen Brighton spying on us. It was the most updated part of the building, maybe even in the entire town. A kitchen table with barely enough chairs for all of us. The other three council members stood while my brothers, Venus, Brighton, and I sat. This was where clan business was discussed, not some converted barroom—the energy in here was too strong. The lower level was for show. The male that had retrieved us when we'd first arrived explained Brighton lived here, but the council was slowly remodeling a house on the opposite side of the block for her.

Brighton made sure to sit next to me while the council was describing the last ten years to Deacon. I scooted my chair away from her as much as possible. Venus had sat on the other side of Steel, and she was acting as if the space I took up was nothing but a black hole that she couldn't see or hear.

What had I said to piss her off?

I had asked for time. I wanted no one but her, and I trusted my brother to have my back. We were all about upholding our ways. But he'd almost lost the love of his life because of a contract stating who he should spend his life with. I couldn't imagine him turning around and doing the same thing to me.

Did Venus think that would happen?

Did she think I would go along with it? Did she think that in my mind, she was nothing but a passing fancy, that I was just another dude bro who wanted to brag about nailing her?

The elder female explained their situation. Her name was Selma, and she hadn't said, but I would guess she'd been the true leader for the last decade.

"We lost Brighton's parents and her older sister in one car accident. As you know, we don't exactly have a foster system in the shifter world. I raised Brighton the best I could—the whole council did."

"But you lack the ability to raise her like she's the future ruler of Garnet clan." Deacon was pointing out the obvious. It would've been prudent to approach Silver clan about a ruler who was in middle school. Instead, they'd tried to hide it, to pretend nothing was wrong.

Selma dipped her head, sadness filling her eyes. "We were unable to teach her some things that would've come naturally to her parents."

It wasn't just the rules and policies. Those could be read in the private tomes the council watched over in city hall. Books that no human would ever see. Members of the council were voted in. Clans held bogus elections to make it look like the ruler was voted mayor, but the city council elections were real. Shifters on the council were normal residents until they were voted in. But ruling families were raised differently than the rest of shifter families. We were raised with innate privilege, a sense of power that everything around us was ours to rule. It didn't matter if a shifter was the firstborn or the third born, the possibility existed, and therefore, we had to be prepared for it.

Children of ruling families had swagger. We were used to getting our way. If we were treated poorly, like in Venus's case, then there was little retaliation when she lashed out. Other shifters would be disciplined. She wasn't. The rest of her clan had probably delighted in her outbursts while she was growing up.

Brighton would've grown up with none of that. She would've deferred to the council for every scrap of knowledge. She probably lacked confidence, and she functioned under a constant state of uncertainty.

Her people would sense that. Our innate aggression would flare, tempted to challenge her.

The family Steel and I had come into contact with had likely capitalized on Brighton's reluctance to kill their oldest son. And then their daughter had gone feral. What would a young shifter like Brighton do? If she tried to carry out a termination and failed, Garnet would lose the last surviving member of the ruling family. And if she won against the male nearly twice her age, she would've had to turn around and take on the sister, also older and more experienced than her.

The council could've stepped in, but with two shifters in their mideighties and the other two in their sixties, perhaps with their own experiences with the family, it had been a lose-lose situation.

Brighton wasn't outwardly aggressive, but she'd already shown she was clever. She flowed and adapted with situations—and I wouldn't put it past her to figure out another way to deal with the ferals.

I rarely talked over Deacon. He might've already pieced this information together, but I had to ask. "Brighton, were you the anonymous caller?"

Her gaze flushed with admiration, and she leaned closer to me. Tentatively, she reached her hand out as if she was going to touch my knee. I scooted to the edge of my chair until I hit the unmoving wall that was Steel.

She withdrew her hand, her expression crestfallen.

"Yes, I didn't know what else to do. I had expected Deacon Silver to come, and I was prepared to propose the solution that I had been thinking about for a long time."

"Long time? Aren't you, like, twenty-one?"

Her smile was serene. Her reddish-brown eyes were lovely, and if she wasn't living under constant fear of being overthrown, she'd probably appear healthier and happier. But I wasn't the guy to do it.

"I'm twenty-three. You're not that much older than me, and when I heard about your brother's mating arrangement and what your council hoped it would do for relations with Jade clan, I got the idea. I just didn't know how to approach it without giving away the precarious position my clan was in."

"While I agree your idea's sound, I am not willing to mate you."

Venus uncrossed one long leg and crossed her other. There was no way she hadn't heard what I said loud and clear.

Hopefulness drained from Brighton's open features. Determination hardened her expression. "You don't even know me, and the ultimate decision is your brother's."

"You would want me even if I was forced to be with you?"

"It's for my clan," she said in a militant tone. "I owe them a chance."

"At the cost of your happiness?"

"I am the last of the bloodline of the first Garnet ruling family. I'm not going to be the legacy that leaves my people in turmoil. And that's what will happen if you don't accept me."

"But why me?" I was sitting next to my single brother. I didn't want to force Steel to be with anyone, but if she was so determined to mate a Silver brother, then why was she focused on me?

"You're closer to my age."

"Age doesn't matter to some of us."

Steel grunted like the idea of being with a female ten years his junior mattered to him. Did he have someone else he'd rather be with? My brother was fast approaching thirty-five but hadn't acted worried.

"I'll have to talk privately to my brothers about this." Deacon rose. He gave the room a dismal scan before he started for the door, expecting us to follow. Venus was the first behind him, and if it wouldn't have made a scene, I would've pushed past Steel to get next to her.

At least we had a two-hour drive back to Avril's place so I could talk to her.

TWELVE

enus

ONCE ALL THE doors were shut in Deacon's pickup, and we drove out of city limits, Penn spoke first. "What the hell was that?"

"I think that was the part she was honest about," Deacon answered. "She used us to deal with the ferals when she might've been killed by them, and because it would've drawn us here where she could propose the mating contract."

I glowered out the window. As much as I wished I was a part of this conversation, yet far away, it wasn't for me. I wasn't part of Silver clan, and none of the answers I had given Penn were yes. He had no contract with my brother. He could do anything he wanted.

And didn't that enrage me?

"Venus." Penn was watching me. The touch of his gaze was like a caress down my cheek. "Talk to me."

"I have nothing to talk about." I kept my tone flat, locking the hostility behind an iron gate. "You asked for more information and you got it."

"Is that what you're mad about?"

"I'm not mad." The stench of my lie rose in the cab. "All right, fine. You chase me eight hours away from home, claiming to want to be with me, and then as soon as some young thing throws herself at you, you're all 'let's take a step back and think about this.'"

Deacon and Steel exchanged a glance, but otherwise stayed silent. Prudent of them to stay out of it. I wanted to hear what Penn had to say as much as I wanted him to keep his traitor mouth shut.

"I was buying time, V. I don't want her. The only female who's captured my interest is you. The only reason I've ever been with anyone else is because you were supposed to be with my brother. But now is my chance, and I want you."

I crossed my arms and twisted in my seat. His face was all harsh angles. The usual jovial, carefree expression he wore was gone. Worry darkened his blue eyes and his jaw was set. My anger wavered. "And if I decide not to be with you, then you'll agree to contract yourself to her? For the good of the people?" Sarcasm dripped out of my lips.

"That's not fair, and you know it. In fact, I think that was the point of your question. You're looking for any and every reason to give up on me." He leaned across the seat, putting his face close to mine. Only pride kept me from backing away. "What if I get fed up at some point? What if I say fine, V, you're right? I can see that you don't want me, and I'm going to back off? That seems to be what you want. What would you do if it happened?"

I ground my teeth together because I didn't know what to say. Panic flaring inside me like a thousand fireworks nearly made me undo my seat belt and fling myself in his arms. To make it worse, we had two witnesses on what should be a very private conversation. I liked Deacon and Steel. They had been civil to me growing up, and after becoming friends with Ava, I would count the two brothers as my friends. But they didn't need to see the most vulnerable part of me.

And Penn, damn him, seemed to glean all the worry from my expression. "Just think about it, V." He held my gaze as he aimed his question at his brother. "Steel, can Venus and I have the house? Can you give us some time to talk tonight?"

"Consider it yours for the night," Steel said without looking back. Both brothers in the front seat stared straight ahead. If they could melt through the floorboards and escape this entire conversation, I thought they would.

"We'll discuss this tonight." Penn kept his voice low. "Only you have the power to turn me away, Venus. I don't give a fuck what Deacon orders me to do. If you say you want me, then I'm yours."

∾

PENN

. . .

129

I DIDN'T THINK Venus would get out of the pickup when Deacon dropped us off at the house, but she slid out without a word and stomped to the door.

I let us in and she marched to the living room, but stalled when her gaze landed on the couch. Even after the drama of the afternoon, my persistent erection was back. Maybe it would be a condition I suffered from the rest of my life while I pined for a female who decided I wasn't worth the effort.

Might as well get right to it. "Did you have time to think?"

She whirled on me, an undefinable emotion lit her green eyes. With her blonde hair behind her shoulders and her nearly glowing green gaze, she looked like the magical creature she was. "I really hate being jealous. I hate being put in the position where I look like a fool in front of everyone. I grew up like that, Penn. You know they call this Envies, and it was for good reason. My parents tried to teach my brothers and I that what others had should be ours by right. They tried to breed jealousy into us, and by some miracle, it didn't take. So instead, they settled for insulting me. For berating me. For making me envious of the intelligence everyone else seemed to have that I didn't. And all that came rushing back standing in that room when you said 'let's take a minute.'"

I wanted to grab her by the shoulders and somehow transfer my energy into her so she could see that I'd never intentionally make her feel less than anything but the strong, smart, amazing shifter she was. I settled for getting as close to her as possible without causing her to back away from me.

"Have you known me to be a liar?"

She clenched her teeth together but shook her head.

"Have you known me to be deceptive—about anything, not just my feelings for you?"

She hugged herself and shook her head again.

"So this is it, V. Are you going to give me a chance or not? Because if you reject me, I'm still a Silver. I don't lead like Deacon. I don't serve and protect like Steel. I don't even have a job right now. So to answer your question, yes. I would mate her. Because you would be gone, and I would continue to be useless."

Some of her defensiveness ebbed. "You feel useless?"

Dammit. I didn't want to get into my hang-ups. They were minor compared to hers. I'd had an easy childhood. My ability in school was revered. Steel was our law, and Deacon was the judge, and I taught online where kids bitched about me. "Yeah, I do. And before you think I'm distracting myself with you, I'm not. Our union would be good for our colonies, but it's unnecessary. It's just what I had to get you to take me seriously."

She drew her lower lip between her white teeth. I had to rip my gaze away. We were baring our souls, not our bodies.

"How dare I be so selfish, Penn? A guy like you wants to be with me, but you're generous enough to want to help a clan that put you in harm's way and got you hurt. You're selfless enough that you want to help Deacon because he has Ava now. Who am I to stop that? You're afraid of being worthless to your people, but you have so many gifts aside from your last name. And I have nothing."

Vulnerability. That was the emotion making her eyes light. She had learned to hide it in every other part of her life, but I could see her. "One of my neighbors is Ellis Stone."

Confusion with the sudden change of subject rippled through her features, but her mouth lifted in a small smile. "I do her hair. She says only I can get the perfect shade of lavender."

"Her mate died five years ago. I was afraid one day I would discover her dead. She was listless, like she had nothing to live for despite having three kids and five grandkids. And one day, she shows up with purple hair. I told her she was killing it, and she gushed over your ability. I don't know how long it took you to do her hair, but it wasn't the color. The time you spent with her gave her her life back."

"I remember when she walked in. I asked her if she had a death wish, an elderly Silver female in Jade territory. But she said one of my other clients is in her bunko group—I think more of our clans mingle than we know—and she wanted to try something new. The appointment took an hour and a half. She talked, and I listened."

"Listening is a rare quality. And you're invaluable to me. If we took everybody out of the equation, what would you want?" I wanted to ask her what she deserved, but I knew she would cower behind that wall. She wouldn't think she deserved anything when she was one of the most deserving individuals I knew.

She chewed her bottom lip, slaying me slowly with hints of her sharp teeth. "If no one else was in the equation, I would want you. The way you make me feel is..." She let out a heavy breath and her gaze touched all the surfaces of the room before landing on me. "The way you make me feel is how I wish I would've been treated my entire life."

"I swear to you that's the only way I want to make you feel."

"Can we pretend that there's no one else but us tonight?"

I couldn't spend what I knew would be a spectacular night with her and know that she wouldn't be mine in the morning. I couldn't do that to myself, and she might not see it the same way, but I couldn't do that to her either. "No, V. What I want with you would last a lifetime, not just one night."

Regret, loss, and disappointment shone in her eyes. "I admire you, Penn, in so many ways. I admire your brains and your conviction. I admire your loyalty. And I'll take the way I feel about you to my grave. Because the sad fact is, we're both dragon shifters from ruling families. And there's more than just me and you involved in this decision now." She poked the middle of her chest. "The only thing keeping me away from you before was pride. And as selfish as it was, I did it to protect me. But I can't put my happiness in front of an entire clan. So tonight is all I can offer you."

I thought I could play hardball. I thought we could talk it out and decide. And deep down, a large part of me thought she would choose me. But she shattered me.

And I would clean up the scraps of myself and hand them over to her, if just for tonight. "Then we'd better not waste it."

THIRTEEN

enus

I LAUNCHED myself into his arms and smashed my mouth on his. He responded instantly. His strong arms banded around me. He wasn't that much taller than me, and I was a big girl, but I hooked my ankles around his waist. As soon as my feet were off the floor, he walked us to the bedroom. He laid me in the middle of the bed, coming down on top of me without breaking the kiss.

The erection I had seen the other night but hadn't gotten to experience was smashed between us. I couldn't go through another day not knowing what being with Penn was like.

Once he broke the kiss, we became a flurry of arms and legs, straining and tearing at our clothing to get it off as soon as possible. I didn't know if he yanked my shirt off or if I helped him. I kicked my shorts to the floor, but I couldn't recall if I also stripped his off. The result was all that mattered.

When we were finally skin to skin, he slowed. He stared into my eyes and brushed long strands of hair off my face. "We might not get any sleep tonight."

"I hope not," I said, my voice breathy.

His smile made the blue of his eyes a few shades brighter. He placed a lazy kiss against my lips and shifted his hips until the broad crest of his erection pushed inside.

Usually, I required some preparation. Like a brunette who wanted to go blonde, there was a process. But not tonight. I was wetter than I had ever been.

I rocked my hips to take him deeper inside. The harsh angles of his face deepened from the strain of holding back.

"Let yourself go, Penn. I can take it."

"I want to fuck you so hard, and I don't want to quit."

"Then do it."

I was going to crawl out of my skin if he held back any longer. Lust fogged my mind, but at the same time, added clarity. Penn and I had a rare chemistry that couldn't be found with just anyone.

As he shoved the rest of the way inside me, filling me completely, our hips flush, I knew I wouldn't experience this again. I had tonight, and that was all. I didn't want to think too far ahead; I didn't want to think beyond my birthday. There was a giant gaping hole beyond that date, but whatever happened, I would have this. I would know what it was like to be treated like I was special. Like he couldn't get enough of me. I would know what it was like when someone I respected and admired treated me with respect and admiration in return. And I had done nothing to deserve it. I was just existing when Penn and I crossed paths two weeks ago. I had coasted through life, waiting for my fate.

Then he had barged into my world after claiming to have patiently waited outside my door for years. He had kept his distance until he realized he no longer had to. And he'd gotten through to stubborn old me.

I would hate myself later. I would rage when I thought about how I delayed his advances while simultaneously being proud of myself for being unselfish, unlike my parents.

He backed out and thrust in. Pleasure ignited every nerve ending in my body, swelling and pulsing until I didn't know where I stopped being Venus and I became the best version of myself with Penn.

Our hands were everywhere. I couldn't quit touching him, and I wanted to memorize the planes of his body under my fingertips. I wanted to cement into my memory the way his abs clenched and relaxed as he moved in and out of me. I wouldn't forget the trail of hair from his lower abdomen leading to where we were connected. Everywhere I could reach, I committed to memory. The soft strands of his hair sliding through my fingers. The way his jaw moved as he claimed my mouth as deliberately as he was claiming me. I knew every part of him I could reach.

"Fuck, V. Next time, I will make it last, I promise."

My toes were already curling, and my knees were drawing up. Delicious tension spread through my body. "Come with me, Penn." I balanced precariously at the precipice of my climax a moment before I catapulted over.

I clamped around him, inside and out. His body went tight between my legs and in my embrace. The heat of his release bonded us together, enhancing the waves of pleasure buffeting between us.

It wasn't until I started floating down from my peak that I realized I'd been yelling into his ear. He had tucked his face into my neck, and he was breathing hard. A spike of fear made me tighten momentarily. He lifted his head, and when his teeth were safely away from my neck, I relaxed. But sizzling disappointment was left behind.

I had been as ambivalent about my claiming as I had about the mating part of my life. They went together, and since I had grown up thinking I wouldn't get a say in who my mate was, I hadn't given any thought to my claiming bite.

Until Penn's mouth was at my neck. And I realized that one of the only things I would ever desperately want in my life was his bite at my neck, but because of who we were, it could never be.

PENN

THE EARLY RAYS of dawn shone into the bedroom. After I had taken Venus three times, I carried her to the shower —our fourth time. And we had collapsed clean and sated into bed.

Neither of us had gotten much sleep, but while my

mind slumbered, my body knew who was lying next to me. I was woken by my throbbing hard-on. Venus's ass pressed into my side, and I was boosting the covers like I could pitch a ten-person tent.

She stirred next to me, coming awake with a soft groan as she stretched her limbs. I didn't realize I had more blood to spare, but it rerouted to head south.

She rolled over to blink at me. God, what a sight. Her blonde hair was tousled. I had never seen it in such a state of disarray. She rarely wore a lot of makeup, but the cheek she slept on was pinker than the other, and her lips were a shade lighter than they were during the day.

I branded her image into my brain. I wouldn't forget this. Any of it. I didn't know how I could be with someone else.

So I refused to think about it. I had gotten this far, doggedly pursuing her one day at a time. It had brought us here, and while I told her I would give up if she said the word, and she had said so many words, I wasn't sure what I would do.

As if she saw the heaviness in my gaze, she walked her fingers over my chest.

"It's not technically the start of the day." Her touch grew bolder.

"It's barely dawn." My voice was gruff but hopeful. We weren't done yet. I held my breath as she dragged the sheet farther down my body.

"I'm never up at dawn."

It was too easy to justify more time together. That had to be a sign. "Then the night isn't done yet."

She flashed me a sexy grin before dragging the sheet all the way off my hips and straddling my legs. Her bare ass was in the air and her head was over my crotch, her lips inches away from the drop of precum glistening on the tip of my erection.

She flicked her tongue and licked it off. A ragged moan left me, and if I wasn't already laying down, I would've collapsed.

Last night, I had buried myself in her as much as possible, but I hadn't tasted her again. Now her mouth was on me, sucking me deeper into the warm depths of her throat. Watching her taste me was a torturous pleasure.

I gave everything to her. She licked and sucked, and I was helpless to do anything but last as long as I could. I alternated between burying my hands in her hair and fisting the sheets when I feared my grip would get too rough. My gaze was riveted on the heart shape her ass made in the air.

I could let go. I could explode into her mouth right now. But I wanted her coming with me.

"Come here," I said more harshly than I intended.

She stopped, her mouth coming off me with a pop, her gaze questioning.

I shifted away from the headboard. "Bring that ass here. I want you on my face."

Her pupils dilated and her exhale of understanding blew over my cock. Excruciating ecstasy.

She did as I had asked. I placed my face between her thighs, and with an iron grip, I buried myself in her folds. Her sharp inhale turned into a gasp and she rocked herself over my tongue. Then that wicked mouth closed back over me.

I wasn't surprised being with Venus was better than I

could've imagined. And I had imagined a lot. In the dark of night, when there was no one else to see that I fantasized about the forbidden female in my life, I had dreamed. I hadn't even tapped the list of things I wanted to do to her.

One night wasn't enough.

I devoured her, drinking her down as I haphazardly thrust into her mouth. We were both growing rough, erratic, and neither of us cared. We were still somehow in sync.

My balls tightened until they were almost painful. I couldn't hold back anymore, and the way she trembled over me, neither could she.

I closed my lips over her swollen clit and sucked, and I just fucking let go. She bucked over my face and the way it made her mouth jerk over my hard length did me in. I exploded, losing all sense of myself and what I was doing. I was nothing but an orgasmic beast with the most beautiful female in the world sitting on my face. This moment was damn near perfect.

She collapsed to the side, and I rolled with her, extracting myself from between her addicting heat. I kept one arm wrapped under her legs and my other hand rested on her hip as we caught our breath and enjoyed the afterglow.

"That tongue of yours, Penn." She had to swallow to catch her breath. "I could listen to you lecture for hours because I know your secret. That tongue is deadly."

This might be the last hour I had with the only female I'd ever wanted in my life, but I chuckled. My laughter grew, and she giggled. After all we'd done together, this was the purest moment between us.

After the hardest of the laughter passed, I sighed. "I won't give up, Venus."

"It'll be easier if you do," she said softly.

I flipped around and rolled her onto her back. We still had time, and I wasn't done with her body. "We'll see about that. Until then, I'm taking what's mine." And I drove inside of her.

FOURTEEN

enus

I LEFT Penn's place when he'd been in the shower. I was a dragon shifter who had saved him from a dank cellar, killing two shifters to do it. Yet I had snuck out of his rental house like a spineless coward and was back at Avril's, sitting in her house alone. I had to wait until she had gone to work again before I could call Lachlan. He answered with a growl.

Spilling the details of what happened the previous day, I kept my emotions out of it as much as possible. Until I got to that part. If I could shift into my dragon and rampage through the forest or pillage an unsuspecting village, it wouldn't dent the rage gusting through my mind and body.

When I was done, Lachlan took a few moments to think about it. He was conscientious like that, almost taking too long to respond to people. A byproduct of being raised by our parents. This was one way he refused to be like them.

"And Penn is set on you?"

"I told him no."

"But he wants you?"

"He can make all the oaths and promises he wants, but if I say no, then they mean nothing."

Lachlan let out a gusty sigh. I could picture him sinking his head into his hand, his dirty blond hair sticking between his fingers. "The thing is, Venus. It's going to look like two Silver brothers passed you over. That's not a good look for Jade."

"You won't have to put up with the bad PR for long."

"Maybe I don't want my sister to fucking die."

I snapped my mouth shut and stared at the large white circles printed on Avril's black rug. This was the second time Lachlan expressed displeasure with the decision I was making. He did what he could to provide for me, but I assumed it was out of a sense of duty. It would look bad for him if one of his siblings didn't appear to be living her best life. Even as our mother and father trashed our trust and loyalty, they still put on a good show for the clan. They might've agreed with all the kids who teased me, but I was still expected to defend myself. Lachlan also fought for me. So did Ronan. I had assumed he'd done it out of obligation. But we were siblings, and he wasn't a guy who showed that he cared.

I was hurting him. Acid ate its way up my throat. I tried to explain the best I could. This wasn't about me. It wasn't even about him. "It's for the best. You should see how bad Garnet River is. They need help, and a link with Silver would do it. Deacon would be justified in giving them aid. And with Penn's innovation, the town could really thrive." I hadn't turned Penn down for no reason.

I hadn't.

"Do you like him?" Lachlan asked. "You said you were giving him a chance, but do you want him?"

"Penn is a really good guy."

"All the Silver brothers are golden boys. You know that's not what I'm asking. Would you mate Penn?"

"You know it's for the best—"

"Goddammit, Venus. That's not what I'm asking, and you know it. You, me, and Ronan have suffered enough. I'm determined to be nothing like our parents, but I'm not above playing a little dirty to get you what you want."

I blinked, once again rendered speechless. This was a side to Lachlan I hadn't seen before. "How dirty?"

I squeezed my eyes shut. What was that question about? My mind hadn't changed. I was the one who told Penn it would be easier just to let go. And here I was, not letting go.

"I'll exploit every rule, law, and policy in our favor." A growl echoed over the phone. "Besides, I don't like this. It's not like you."

"How so?"

"You don't fight unless you have to, Venus, but you also don't give up. Yet you're giving up, and you're not fighting."

"I told you why."

"And on the surface, it sounds good. Look deeper. Penn is a Band-Aid for Garnet. The solution you're supporting breeds out the issue. Put a Silver in charge. He'll teach their young how to lead."

I frowned. The way Lachlan described it sounded messed up.

He continued. "Think about it. If I had died with our parents, and you took over, what would've gotten you to mate when you didn't want to?"

"How do we know she doesn't want to? Penn is hot, and he's got a nice hoard." That sounded dirty, but if Penn's hoard was as large as his cock, then he was financially secure. "I would've either stepped down to mate Deacon since we couldn't mate if both of us were rulers, or I would've stayed single."

"And what about if you were challenged?"

Our parents had set me up so that if I had ever risen as ruler, I would've been immediately challenged. "I would've fought. And I would've won."

Winning or death would've been my only option. Surviving under another ruler would have been a traumatic experience for a defeated female.

Oh.

"You think Brighton is afraid of being challenged?" She should be. She didn't look like she could take on a butterfly and come out the victor. How had she not been challenged yet?

There was a reason. Just like there was more going on with Brighton.

"If what you said about her is true, she might not fear the challenge, but she's damn sure she's going to lose. But that's not your problem, is it?"

I bit my cheek at Lachlan's cavalier but pointed remark. It wasn't my problem, but I empathized with her. And he'd pointed out how easily I had given up without thinking things through—just like my parents had wanted. "I need to talk to Deacon." And Penn. "Thank you, Lachlan. I'm glad you don't hate me."

"You're surrounded by people that care about you.

You can thank me by noticing that."

I had grown up feeling alone, but I'd had my brothers. I'd gone my adult life feeling alone, but I'd had my brothers and my clients. And now, I had Ava, and Avril, and the Silver brothers.

I sent Deacon a message. I needed to talk to him. My stomach flipped and twirled like it was getting ready to go to a ball and meet Prince Charming. How was I going to face Penn after the way I'd left him?

You don't fight unless you have to, Venus, but you also don't give up.

I wasn't giving up. And that might mean it was time to fight for what I wanted.

$\sim$

PENN

DEACON AND AVA came over to the house after some message from Venus telling him we needed to talk more. The female left my head spinning. She'd given me one night with her and left without saying goodbye. And now she was calling all of us together again.

Venus walked in without knocking. Her long hair was gathered into a bun at the top of her head, baring the neck I wanted to bite. I'd had so many chances to put my mark there. I'd never do it without her approval, but it was one of the many fantasies I still harbored about her.

Her gaze sought mine, and she offered an apologetic smile. I dipped my head, but our interaction didn't help me figure out what was going on.

She didn't waste time on chitchat. "My brother

brought up some interesting points. If I had become Jade's ruler in my early twenties, I would've been challenged before the sun had set. So instead of thinking that her request is a good political move, why aren't we asking why hasn't she been challenged yet?"

Steel frowned, balancing precariously on a kitchen chair with his boots on the table. "She had to have been taught to fight. She was young when her parents died, but the council would've continued."

Deacon tucked Ava into his side on the couch. "The clan might support her."

I shook my head, my mind working through Venus's points. "We're progressive, but aren't that far along that a bunch of aggressive creatures, especially the males, would take orders from a lone young female."

"She has the council," Deacon said, but he wasn't arguing. His tone was distant, like he was trying to puzzle out the answers. "Her parents might've been well liked, but the clan wasn't thriving under them either. There has to be someone in that clan convinced they can do better. But they haven't made their move. Why?"

It was obvious what Garnet would have to gain by mating me with Brighton. Power. Money. Prestige. It would take years, decades even, to build the town back up, but the quality of life of each shifter in the clan would improve sooner than if they'd done it on their own. Gem hoards or not, our clans needed to be independent and find their own strength. Brighton was using me for strength.

Venus's brother was right. Mating me wasn't the answer. But how would we learn what was really going on in order to help them—or let them suffer a natural fate?

We had to get them talking. The council was old enough to know when to keep their mouths shut. Brighton was so damn young she made me feel ancient. But she was the best route to take, and a plan formed in my mind.

"Let me preface this by saying I don't like this idea." I had everyone's attention. "Let me meet with Brighton."

"On a date?" Venus's tone was an acid that ate through the connection between us.

"She would think it was a date. I vow I will do nothing else with her but talk."

Silence fell around the room. If Brighton threw herself at me and rained kisses down on my skin, I would have broken a vow. Deacon would be within his right to carry out my punishment. But I didn't want to risk my chances with Venus.

"I can get her alone, away from the council. She sees me as more of an equal and she might talk more freely."

"You think you'll be able to get a female to do that by *talking* on one date?" Venus's skeptical tone told me she hated the idea.

"It may take more." I suppressed a wince. When she said it like that, it sounded like I planned to seduce Brighton, or that I would have to fake a relationship. For me, it wouldn't be real, but I didn't like the thought of leading someone on, and doing it with Venus as an observer.

Deacon rubbed his chin between his thumb and his forefinger. "I think Penn's idea might be the best way to move forward."

"We need to find out," Steel agreed.

I looked to Venus, but she held her hands up in the universal signal of *staying out of it*.

"Do it," Deacon said. "We just need to get her talking."

"Give me her contact information and I'll set it up." Keeping my mind on business, I turned to Venus. "Can I get your advice?"

Her tone was flat when she answered. "You want my advice on how to date Brighton Garnet?"

Frustration made me want to gnaw my hand off and offer it to Venus as collateral. She wouldn't have to give it back if I fucked up. "I'm not dating her. If I was honest, I'd think sending you would work better. Look at how you won over Ava and Avril. You have a better chance at earning Brighton's trust than I do."

Venus crossed a long leg as if she needed to suppress her shock. "Why does everyone think I'm such a people person all of a sudden?"

"Because we didn't pay attention before," Deacon answered. "You had Ava's father telling you everything about his life the first time you met him."

Steel dropped his boots from the table. "Don't get me wrong, Penn can do a lot of things. But he's used to females throwing themselves at him. And he's used to them running when he starts rambling."

"I'm not that bad, jackass."

He rolled his eyes. "You're not making any woman spill their secrets by telling them why the sky is blue."

The Raleigh scattering phenomenon was a cool topic and I could explain it rather quickly.

"You're thinking of the answer, aren't you?" Steel asked.

I shot him a dirty look, but nodded.

"Venus, he needs help, unless you're willing to date her."

Venus spread her fingers as if she was studying the green polish on her nails. "She won't talk to me. I'm too much older than her. She's more likely to relate to Penn without an already established friendship. Otherwise, she might suspect Jade wants to take advantage of her situation." She chewed on her lower lip and fisted her hand. "Honesty is your best bet. Steel was onto something. If she tries to throw herself at you and gets rebuked, she might not trust your intentions either."

"So I should tell her I don't want to mate her, but that I want to help?" I could've done that when we were in Garnet River.

"I think that's the best, yes, but don't lead with that. Just get to know her. She's probably been isolated her whole life. She's lonely, and she's scared. She needs a friend more than she needs a mate, and she thinks she really needs you as a mate."

"Gah." Ava shook her head. "Now I feel bad for her."

Deacon and Steel murmured back and forth, but I held Venus's gaze, wishing we were the only two in the room. "You're really something, you know that."

"I'd like to hear you explain why the sky is blue." She dropped her gaze like a shy girl who'd just asked a boy out.

Steel snorted and got up. "You'd better make this date, Penn. Because you're not finding that in just anyone."

I ignored him and leaned toward the female I wanted to be mine forever. "Next time, don't sneak out and I'll tell you."

"Is there going to be a next time?"

"Yes." I caught her green eyes and absorbed as much of the insecurity I saw there as possible. "I promise."

CHAPTER
FIFTEEN

 enus

I NEVER HAD THIS EXPERIENCE. I never anticipated needing it. Cartons of half-empty ice cream lined the coffee table, interspersed with bags of various flavored M&M's. Penn had made a promise. He'd made two of them. I trusted him. But I also had emotions that didn't give a damn what Penn said, he was with another female right now.

Ava put the lids on the two cartons closest to her. "I don't have your metabolism, Venus. I need to stop or I'm gonna puke all over Deacon when I crawl into bed."

I snorted. "Bet he wouldn't mind."

Avril snickered and dug into her chocolate chip cookie dough. "Ain't that the truth? He'll probably tell you how sexy you look as he cleans it up for you."

"Gross!" Ava dissolved into laughter.

This was exactly what I had needed. What would

tonight have been like if I had done nothing but sit alone and wonder what Penn and Brighton were doing?

"Guys? When did I fall this hard for a male ten years younger than me?"

Avril cocked her brow and gave me a look that said *you seriously don't know?* "Since he's a guy that looks like Penn. I think that's pretty self-explanatory. You practically oozed into the house yesterday morning. That was no walk of shame—because you could barely walk."

Ava let out a theatrical gasp and collapsed backward. "My innocent ears."

"I'm sure you know exactly what she's talking about, Ava." I traded in my empty carton of ice cream for the mint M&M's. Might as well get a gut ache and have fresh breath.

"They are brothers after all," Avril tacked on.

I didn't mean to take the serious route, but that was what my next question did. "What do you think they're doing? It's not like there's anywhere to go in Garnet River."

"He borrowed Steel's pickup." Ava sat up, all remnants of humor wiped from her face. "There's a town close by, right?"

"Yes, and it has a little diner." I shoved a handful of candy in my mouth.

Avril stretched her arms high overhead. She had changed out of her scrubs at the hospital. She had run to the grocery store for our emergency girls' night supplies. We were all dressed the same—shorts with elastic waistbands and loose T-shirts.

I polished off my goodies and began gathering our snacks off the end table. I had more activities planned.

Anything to keep my mind busy. "I brought my mani-pedi travel kit."

Avril's face lit up before she schooled her expression. "Don't you do that for a living? I can't imagine it's something you want to do on your vacation."

Technically, this wasn't my vacation. It was supposed to be my last month of freedom before I was terminated. It was me running from Penn. And look where that got me. Vacation or not, I enjoyed making people feel good. They relaxed in my salon when I had seen them do nothing but tense around my family. "I enjoy doing them. I really like my job."

Avril pinched the bridge of her nose and her jaw shuddered like she was suppressing a yawn. "I could go for some job fulfillment. I've only been at this for three years, but I'm run ragged."

"Are you going to apply at the clinic?" Ava asked.

Avril shook her head, her dark ponytail swinging. "It's not what I got into nursing to do. I want to work in the hospital. It is just the constant state of go I can't take. Running on all cylinders for twelve hours, shift after shift after shift. I don't know if I'm going to last to collect my pension."

"I'm sorry," Ava murmured. "Venus, I think Avril gets the pedicure first."

I jumped up and ran downstairs to the guest room. A minute later, I was back with my foot bath and my tackle box of supplies. "I'll move the coffee table. You can stay sitting where you are."

I went into work mode. My mind wasn't on me, it was on my client. I wanted Avril to relax, to be pampered, to rediscover a part of herself that had been buried under obligation and duty.

Ava curled her legs under her and leaned against the armrest of her recliner. She was next. "I know you just told us you enjoy your job, Venus. But you're great at it. Did you really think you weren't a people person?"

I dried off Avril's feet as I thought about the conversation at the house when Penn asked me for advice. I shoved a tray of polish in Avril's hands. "Pick out a color." I thought about what Ava said. "I never thought of myself that way, I guess."

"You've known everyone in Jade Hills and Silver Lake your entire life," Ava said. "They pigeonholed you into one identity. Even Deacon talked about you differently, and when I met you, I was surprised how wrong he was."

"I'm sure he was more accurate than you think."

"Maybe he was accurate for twenty years ago. You're allowed to change."

I gave her an amused smile, but it was also a cover for talking with someone about myself. Ava was being complimentary, but she also saw a lot being a new arrival in my life. "How are you so wise for being so young?"

She laughed. "It's all that life insurance I sold. People told me their life stories."

She was easy to talk to, and so refreshingly young that she hadn't yet bought into everything that had been told to her. "I haven't changed, but I surround myself with people who don't treat me poorly. That was my biggest goal for adulthood. I was still a Jade, and I had to stay close to home for my brothers." I modified my explanation in time for Avril. "I have my own place, my own business, and life is good."

Avril handed me the Midsummer Night's Storm shade of polish. "That's why you had to get away when

Penn started pursuing you. He would upset the tidy life you've built for yourself."

Why bother to deny it? "Yep." I held the bottle of polish up to the light. "This is the color of Steel's eyes, don't you think?"

Ava squinted and studied the color. It must've been hard for her to pay attention to the color of Steel's eyes while she was lost in Deacon's gaze.

"Oh, really? I didn't notice." Avril's tone was deceptively innocent.

Thanks to my years of experience with clients, I shrugged and gave the polish a shake. If Avril didn't want to admit to us or herself that she chose the color because it reminded her of Steel, then I wouldn't be the one to call her out. I spent most of the conversation trying not to talk about Penn, but getting drawn in. For my friend, I would take one for the team.

"It would be hard for any of the blues not to remind me of Penn's eyes. His color changes depending on his mood."

Ava wiggled out of the recliner to grab the tray of various polishes. "Would it be too weird if I chose a silver?"

"You're a newlywed," Avril answered quickly, like she was grateful to move on from a subject that had anything to do with Steel. "You're allowed to be sappy. Remember when we did both our hands and our feet in black when we were freshmen?"

I concentrated on putting the polish on Avril's toes, marveling over how the color matched Steel's eyes even better on her. Was it a sign?

I wouldn't worry about anyone else's love life, so I

lost myself in listening to Avril and Ava's stories of their high school years.

I had just found them. Friends that I could trust. Friends that dropped everything to help each other and me. I didn't want to lose it, just like I didn't want to lose Penn now that he got through to me.

~

PENN

EVERYTHING FELT WRONG. The landscape was wrong. It was similar to the Turtle Mountains, but the trees were a little bigger and the roads were windier. The smells were wrong. The river that ran by the town didn't have the fresh lake smell of Silver Lake. And the person I was with didn't have a scent that reminded me of white chocolate dribbling over a bowl of ice cream, with the faint undertones of nail polish and hair product.

Brighton Garnet didn't smell like Venus; she certainly didn't smell bad. But to my brain, her scent might as well be like a sewer.

When I called to set up this not-a-date, I had asked Brighton if she wanted to go to the neighboring town. There was a bar and grill and a small diner we could eat at. But Brighton had insisted on a picnic. The idea of a picnic was too romantic for my taste, but she might talk easier in private, so I had volunteered to pack the picnic supplies.

I packed enough to ensure we filled our bellies. Deacon had consulted with Silver Lake's council and poured over the information they had on Garnet River.

The clan had shunned all aid programs, preferring to starve their people rather than use resources meant to help in their situations.

When we reached the camping area at a bend in the river, Brighton took great care in spreading out the blanket I had packed. She laid out the food along one edge, leaving the other half-open for the two of us to cram onto. Forced proximity.

Venus's advice was at the forefront of my mind. I wasn't seducing Brighton. I wasn't even tricking her into trusting me. She needed a friend, and sharing that blanket would make her think I was interested when I wasn't.

I chose the supreme sub and wandered to the edge of the water as I munched on it. Brighton's gaze burned on my back, so different from Venus's. The effect was weaker, less direct, and my inner dragon didn't thump its tail and dream of all ways to taste Brighton.

"Good fishing in the river?" I asked.

"I don't fish."

Who lived this far in the country and didn't hunt or fish? Our nature made us want to procure food in ways that didn't include self-checkout. "It would help with the food supply."

She bristled, rubbing her fingers together like she was trying to get invisible crumbs off. "What makes you think we have a food supply issue?"

Might as well get right down to it. "The grocery store two blocks from city hall was all boarded up. Hale and hearty isn't exactly how I would describe any of the shifters we've seen in your clan. And the fields and pastures tucked into the trees around Garnet River aren't a part of the town. Human farmers and ranchers work the land, not your people." Shit. That might've been the opposite of what Venus recommended.

Her mouth tightened. She straightened her back like someone had shoved a ramrod straight down her spine. "My parents were in the process of buying land for farming and ranching. It was my great-grandparents' dream to move our people to a place where the clan could expand. But it wasn't until my parents' time that these family farms were open for sale. Younger generations wanted more options than what their parents and grandparents had. But by then..."

By then, her parents had been killed in a car accident with her older sister.

"There's gotta be something else you can do." I was sympathetic to her plight. She was younger than me, trying to save an entire clan of people. I wanted to help her, but I didn't want to sacrifice the love of my life to do it.

"Most things take money. We're trying to resurrect this campground, bring in some side hustle money, but it's risky." She punctuated her words with her hands. "These woods are where we can be ourselves, and if we invite a whole bunch of humans in, and someone gets busted in their dragon form, I would take responsibility for it. I can maybe wipe a human memory or two, but would it become my full-time job? Would that burn my mind out?"

I was finally seeing the real Brighton. She was young, with a huge amount of responsibility on her slim shoulders. She had very few resources to aid her in her position, and the council was just as hindered as her.

"Why didn't you go to my brother?"

She opened her mouth to answer, then snapped it

shut. Her red-brown eyes stared at the twinkling surface of the river. "You saw your brother's reaction. If he enacted Silver law, then what? He hands the clan back and they're supposed to take me seriously? They already—"

This time, I sensed she wouldn't elaborate. I was getting close to the real challenge this clan faced. I had to keep trying. "My brothers and I can help you think of something, Brighton. You don't have to go through this alone. Now that we know—"

"I'm running out of time." Desperation sharpened the irritated edge to her voice.

Time. My brother had been up against a ticking clock. Venus was in the same situation. And now Brighton. I was the only one who seemed to have a surplus of time.

The hair on the back of my neck stood up. We were being watched. Casually, I chewed a bite from a sandwich as I spun in a relaxed circle, pretending to take in the scenery around me.

Brighton jumped up, her food forgotten.

The stranger we had each sensed ambled out of the woods. He was a shifter, and nude. If he didn't have his clothes, then he was in the trees to shift or go for a swim. This far in the boondocks, it wasn't a big deal that it was broad daylight. But something about the male didn't put me at ease. Between his smugly hostile features and his cocky swagger, I didn't trust that he happened upon us during a casual stroll.

"Camden." Brighton's tone was hard. Her gaze sharpened to two laser beams that tracked the new arrival's every move. "What are you doing here?"

"I heard what you're trying to do, Brighton." Even his tone was arrogant. His white-blond hair was slicked back but the scent coming off of him was male sweat, not had-a-quick-swim-in-the-river. "Trying to whore yourself out because you're too weak to lead my people?"

"It's none of your business." Brighton fisted her hands at her sides. Her defiant stance looked like a five-year-old standing up to an outraged adult. She couldn't take this male in a fight. In their human form, Camden could subdue her in less than ten seconds. In shifter form, he could probably render her limb by limb.

This was the reason Brighton acted the way she did. Camden's proprietary gaze didn't alter whether it was on her or the surrounding land. When he looked at me, it switched to hostile and defensive. But when his pale-blue gaze touched on Brighton, there was ownership.

"Nice day for a shift?" I asked, keeping my voice light.

Resentment boiled over in his frosty gaze. "Neither of us were talking to you, Silver."

"Yet I'm here. You intruded on my picnic; we didn't intrude on your walk."

Camden puffed his chest out. He was my age. Definitely older than Brighton, but not by much. "Are you asking for a fight, Silver? Are you pissed because I ruined your nice little meal with my girl?"

I lifted a brow. The council hadn't mentioned one of their clan's shifters had laid claim on their ruler. "I'm not upset. I am perplexed though." I tilted my head and deliberately regarded him as if he was nothing more than one of my biology specimens. "But it's been a long time since I've been challenged."

My detached calm had the effect I wanted. His confidence wavered. An exhale deflated his chest and uncertainty entered his expression. He fought to achieve the aggression that had been there before he realized I wouldn't back down from a challenge. "I have better things to do than waste my time with a fucking Silver."

"I'm sure you do." I adopted an amused smile, as if the thought of him having important things to do entertained me.

Rage rippled under his skin and he began to change. His bones lengthened and his skin transitioned to green scales.

Perhaps he shifted to look more menacing, but I had seen the way my behavior unsettled him. He couldn't control his emotions, and he shifted to cover it up. In a few seconds, I faced a good-sized green dragon, and it was a good thing he hadn't officially challenged me. He would've found out I was much larger than him. And the silver sheen on my scales would've added another level of intimidation. Not only was I from the clan that ruled all dragon shifter clans, but I had the size and fighting skill to back it up. I had grown up with two older brothers.

He stormed into the trees, creating a ruckus of broken branches and rustling leaves behind him. When he was out of earshot, I turned toward Brighton. She was staring at the ground, her hair hanging in her face. A decidedly undefiant stance that went against how she should act as a dragon shifter ruler.

"How about you tell me what's really going on?"

CHAPTER
SIXTEEN

enus

I LISTENED, my sympathy growing more as Penn talked. He had called his brothers after his time with Brighton and told them he knew what was going on and we should get down there.

Brighton Garnet had put me through a wringer of emotions, but she had unintentionally made me admit I wanted to be with Penn. She'd pushed me into spending a night with Penn that I couldn't recover. I may have walked away from him that morning, but I'd wanted it to be temporary.

And now I was ready to strip off every article of clothing, shift into my dragon, and roar at anyone who tried to get close to her. My mating contract with Deacon had insulated me from males like Camden. Males who thought might made right because we were shifters. Males who'd take what they wanted at the expense of their people. I'd been willing to sacrifice my happiness—my life—for the good of dragon shifter-kind, so Garnet clan could get strong again. And some fucking male wanted to smother the clan in order to call himself ruler?

Not on my watch.

Deacon summarized her situation. "Let me get this straight. The council held Garnet clan together until you turned eighteen. But this male, Camden, and his family have been plotting to take over?"

Brighton nodded and hugged herself. Our kind's rulers were supposed to be the mightiest of the mighty. The ruling families were supposed to be the most cunning, the most ruthless, the most conniving. The underlying theme: they were supposed to be the strongest. And Brighton may have met all those qualifications if her parents hadn't been killed. But she was bounced among the homes of the council members as they struggled to hold the clan together. Camden Miller. And his siblings. His parents. Even his grandparents.

"And he gave you five years," Deacon continued. "In order for Camden to look like a hero, swooping in to rescue the clan, he gave you five years to mess up your position, and then he would challenge you."

"Or agree to mate him. I will not be with that male," Brighton said through clenched teeth. "He'll finish running my people into the ground, or he'll get everyone killed trying. I don't doubt he thinks that gaining my seat in Garnet is only a step closer to challenging your clan."

She wouldn't be with that male, yet she was trying to trick another to be with her. Still, I couldn't fault her logic. If I was in her position, with all my experience fighting, I'd have a hard time taking on an entire family. It was why ruling families often had more than one kid. We were supposed to support each other.

"What have you been doing in the last five years?" Deacon adjusted the way he sat in the threadbare chair he'd sat in the last time we were in the building.

Brighton tied her long hair into a messy bun at the base of her head. She'd gone all out for the date with a low-cut top. Despite how lean she was, she made the most of her cleavage. Her bottoms were as short as her legs were long.

But none of her scent clung to Penn. He'd kept his word. He'd used my advice to get to the bottom of Brighton's situation. Camden's appearance helped speed the process up, but having Penn Silver listen to me about clan politics was a heady experience.

I focused back on what Brighton was saying.

"I looked into federal and state programs for assistance. Same with the county. We could've applied for grants to help remodel some buildings downtown." The red in her eyes sparked. "But the Millers put a stop to that."

"How?"

Brighton rolled her eyes. "Their most effective weapons are their mouths. They talk. They insinuate. They spread misinformation and rumors. As our only local mechanics, they have access to everyone's ear who need engine repair. They foster the reliance, keeping the skills to themselves, and I wouldn't put it past them to sabotage some engines to get more business." Heavy loss darkened the brown of her eyes.

And I knew. "Do you think—"

"Yes." That was all she was going to say, or dared to say, when it came to accusing the Millers of being behind her parents' deaths. She sucked in a breath and resolution filled her eyes. "The rumors that finally reached me came from ten families telling me they'd refuse to use one cent of the money they didn't earn." She leaned forward, her body taut. "They distinctly said they'd rather have their kids die of hunger than lick one food stamp. Meanwhile, the Millers overhunt the woods around us and sell the overage. They steal from my people and then have the audacity to profit from those same people."

And she was one person against an entire family. "Do you know how to fight?" I asked.

Her expression shuttered. "I know some basic techniques."

"That's not enough."

Her reaction was enough. We all knew the basics, and she wasn't confident in her skill with those.

"It was enough when Camden tried to force himself on me the summer after graduation. He still wears the scar on his chest."

"But now he'll be ready." When I'd been training with my brothers, being Jade hadn't seemed like it came with any benefits. But learning to fight like a rabid mountain lion with jock itch was one of them. "I'll work with you."

The guys stared at me. Brighton cocked her head as if to try to hear me better. "Excuse me, what?"

"I'll work with you. It'll look better to work with a female. The Millers can't get misogynistic over that. Silver males aren't swooping in to save you, and I planned to be in the area for another three weeks." Avril would understand when I told her I had a friend in the area who needed a little help. "And you rescind your request to mate Penn." I flicked my gaze to a stunned Penn. "If that's what he wants."

"Yes," he answered immediately.

Guilt weighed down Brighton's expression when she glanced at Penn. "I thought we'd be a good match since we're so close in age. We've all heard about you—wicked smart and teaching at a university online. Silver Lake gets your knowledge when we need teachers in Garnet River so badly."

Penn's shoulders hung from the expectations of his kind. They didn't know he'd lost his job, but from the way his brows drew together, his mind was working. "We can get you the resources you need."

"Absolutely," Deacon added. "We'll cover all of that while Venus works with you. You're in charge, Brighton. We know it. You know it. And before my brothers and I are done here, the Millers are going to good and goddamn well know it."

Brighton's lips trembled, but she tucked her shoulders back. The girl was young, but she was determined. She'd been forged in hard times, and Camden Miller didn't understand what he was facing. She was a sleeping dragon, and I'd make sure she woke the hell up.

PENN

AFTER MEETING WITH BRIGHTON, we'd all gone back to our respective spaces. Steel and I were at the house. Deacon and Ava had gone back to the hotel. Venus was with Avril, talking to her about leaving for a while to help Brighton.

I had dreaded the picnic, but it'd turned the situation around.

I couldn't believe Venus had offered to help Brighton after what she'd done. But now that I knew her, I shouldn't be surprised. She helped others. It was what she did, whether it was my neighbor or the female who tried to steal her boyfriend.

What was I to her? She'd gotten me out of a tough situation. But she hadn't said the magic words. *"Yes, I'll be yours."*

I sprawled on my bed and stared at my phone. Should I call her? If I was to be her mate, I wouldn't hesitate to send messages or dial her up to hear her voice.

I could rattle off the Krebs cycle, but I was lost trying to decide if I should call her.

I'd raced to Minneapolis to win her over before her birthday. Fucking call her.

I dialed before I chickened out.

The sultry way she answered was enough to keep me hard the rest of the night. "Penn Silver. Don't you know that us old people go to bed early?"

"I know full well that you have excellent stamina after midnight."

Her soft chuckle was muffled.

"Is Avril home?"

"Yes, she works at the crack of dawn. I can't believe how she switches back and forth between shifts."

"What did she say when you told her you'd be going to Garnet River?"

"It works out. She'll be on overnights soon, and I would've felt like a pain."

"I'm going with you." I had already told Deacon. I hadn't asked.

"I'll be fine."

"I know, but I want to be close to you, and overseeing Garnet River for Deacon is the perfect excuse."

"What do you think it's going to be like?"

"Camping, and I'm going to pack a lot of food."

She laughed and quickly cut it off. "Sorry. Avril's bedroom is right above me and I don't want to wake her. Brighton said I could use the house the council was updating for her. Do you... want to stay with me?"

"Honey, I was going to sneak into your sleeping bag."

"I was hoping you would." The other end got really quiet for a moment. "I'm sorry for the way I left after we spent the night together."

"V, I don't care how you leave as long as you keep coming back."

"Or you'll come after me?"

"Always."

She still hadn't said the words, but we were so close. I wouldn't fuck it up by pressuring her.

"So while I bring out the badass in Brighton, what are you going to do?"

"Watch your ass and plan what I'm going to do to you the next time I can sink my teeth into it."

"Penn, don't you dare get me hot. I don't want to show up dead tired tomorrow."

"Fine." So phone sex wasn't in the stars tonight. I might have to go out for a run instead. "I'm going to work with the council to learn what capabilities Garnet River has and what we can bring in that won't make them feel like they're a giant charity case, since her clan has been programmed to be resistant to help."

"I know she said her parents moved here to get some distance between them and the other clans, but Peridot clan isn't far away."

"You know how Peridot is. Arrogant as fuck." My brothers and I had dealt with Peridot's ruling family one year and it was like a clan full of Millers. Dragon shifters had a healthy ego. Peridot took it to a new level.

"Right. Even my parents avoided them." The hitch in her breathing told me she was yawning.

"I'll let you go. Pick me up tomorrow?"

"What if I don't?" Her playful tone was the only thing that kept me from camping out on the hood of her car.

"I'll find you."

"You seem good at that, but then you're good at everything."

"Except teaching."

"You'll get that too. But consider this possibility—you might've been teaching just fine, but it's the school that sucks."

"I heard snoring over the video call."

"Okay, the students sucked."

I hadn't thought I'd be able to laugh about my failed career. "Good night, Venus."

"Good night, Penn."

"Hey—before you hang up."

"Yeah?"

"When I go to sleep, I'm going to dream about how I'd make small circles with my tongue until I suck your clit in my mouth because I fucking love when your legs almost burst my skull like a watermelon."

"Penn—that imagery comes close to ruining the dirty talk."

I grinned. "But it didn't."

"No, damn you. So remember that thing with my tongue I did? Keep remembering."

I groaned as she hung up. I might be hard enough to carve my name in a marble statue, but I went to sleep smiling.

CHAPTER

SEVENTEEN

 enus

DRIVING through Garnet River in a red convertible with one of the Silver brothers was the best way to announce my presence. People stopped midconversation when I drove by. It didn't help that I put the top down, had my aviator shades on, and tied a green scarf around my hair.

Penn looked like he was ready to hike a trail or two and do a photo shoot for a sportswear company while he was at it. He wore a white-and-red short-sleeved shirt that could wick moisture as well as repel the sun's heat. His loose tan pants should have trouble blending into the boardroom and the hiking trail but could still work for both. His hiking boots capped off his outfit.

No. The dark locks of hair that stood in all directions from two hours of letting it whip in the wind completed his "I'm gonna teach you some stuff, and it might be outdoorsy, it might be techy, or it could be both" vibe. I was addicted.

I parked in front of city hall and left the top down. Was I itching for a fight? Maybe. Restless energy lined my bones. I hated people like Camden Miller. I'd never met him, but I'd grown up with people like him. My parents were probably worse than his, and they'd have encouraged an entire clan of Millers. Lachlan was slowly and meticulously discouraging that type of behavior, but attitudes had been fostered for generations.

Brighton stepped out of city hall. This time when she eyed Penn, it wasn't with an anticipatory look. She hadn't been interested in mating him, and I doubted she was interested in mating anyone.

"You're here." She scanned each side of the street. A couple was out for a walk. There were two guys who'd just parked a couple of blocks away. Her eyes narrowed on the old farm pickup they drove.

"Are we attracting attention?"

"Yes. I did what you said and didn't tell anyone about your arrival. Only the council knew you were returning, and I required their confidence."

The clan had to learn to trust their ruler. Everyday workings shouldn't concern them. This wasn't a human city. They didn't need to peer over their mayor's fence to ensure he was doing only approved activities. They didn't need to monitor who Brighton spent her time with. If she consulted other clans' ruling families, it wasn't their business. They had to trust that she would make announcements when necessary.

Brighton wasn't voted into office. It only looked like that on paper—for human eyes. She was their leader by birthright, and if her authority was challenged, she had to physically back up her claim.

That was what I was here for.

I unwrapped my scarf. I had braided my hair down each side of my head and twisted the ends into a bun at the back of my neck. The black athletic shorts and green top I wore were easy to strip off—but also highlighted exactly what clan I was from, as if they didn't know already. But it paid to be obnoxious about it, and it was good for Garnet to see more than one clan interacting with their ruler.

Lachlan had agreed. He wasn't the type to apologize for our parents' ways. He preferred action over words. To everyone else, I was here with his permission and that assumption suited both my brother and me just fine. He had no designs on Garnet, and my actions would help prove it.

"Ready to get to work?" I asked.

Brighton's gaze shifted to the two males from the pickup. I didn't look at them, but I gauged Penn's reaction. There was no recognition in his eyes. Neither of the men was Camden, but that didn't mean he didn't have supporters who acted as his eyes and ears. His entire family had likely been recruiting people to their side.

Her expression hardened until she looked like she wanted to rip into the tenderest of flesh of the two guys. Perfect. She needed resting bitch face. Her lost fawn expression wasn't getting her anywhere.

"I'm ready. I'll show you to the house you both can use. It has running water and electricity, and even some basic furniture. Selma hasn't wanted me to live there alone."

Which hadn't added confidence in reference to her ability.

"We'll make it work," Penn said. "Is the council inside?"

She nodded. "They're waiting for you."

Penn gave me one last look before he disappeared inside. When I was alone with Brighton, I flashed her a sunny smile that might've been more than a little predatory. But that wasn't for her benefit.

"Time to train."

"Are we driving there?" She dubiously studied my car. "I don't think that's going to get far on the trails."

"No, we're going to swagger obnoxiously through town and make everyone wonder what the hell you're doing."

A smile ghosted over her lips. "I like that idea more than you know."

I dug my tote out of the car. "Lead the way."

She started for the edge of town in the same direction as the Trevinos' place. After we cleared city limits, I asked her about her training. How much she fought in her human form and what she'd done with her dragon.

"My dragon is..." Her nervous gaze darted around us. We were getting deeper into the trees. No one was around. "Small."

"Then the first thing we have to do is wipe from your mind that you need to be huge to be effective. My mother was a nasty piece of work and she was five-four. My dragon was one and a half times her size, and it made her fight dirtier."

"I've heard stories of your mother."

"Believe them."

"Why aren't you that way?"

"Because in their mind, it was them against the world. My brothers and I were in the world that often had to fight them."

We reached a space that had been cleared by dragon bodies slamming into trees. This must be a popular training area. Enough repeated hits and the trees had buckled and been cleared.

Brighton danced from foot to foot and tipped her head side to side like she was warming up. "My parents were strict, but I don't remember a lot. I thought the world of my sister. She would've been an amazing leader."

"She might've been. But you're it now. Regardless of how or why you have the position, and you know how important it is to keep it. You feel the responsibility. You were willing to mate yourself off to keep your clan alive. That means anyone else fighting for leadership is fighting for themselves. As long as you are motivated by the welfare of your people, you are the leader they need." I dropped my tote of snacks and water and whipped my shirt off. "Let's start with our dragons."

Pure delight infused her face. With her comment on her size, I assumed she didn't shift often. She'd felt too vulnerable. But she was with me, and anyone interrupting our time would incur my wrath. She was safe to shift, and she'd only get stronger.

I'd get to flex my wings. I didn't have the chance to at home. I'd hid in my home and my business. I wasn't that much different from Brighton in that way. She'd been told the last several years of her life that she was the leader but she shouldn't be. I was sure she'd been told how promising her sister had been. All of that fed into her identity.

Just like I'd been told I wasn't worth anything. I wasn't smart enough to be good for anything but a mating contract. I was too old for a guy like Penn.

Fuck all that noise.

Brighton wouldn't be the only one discovering her true potential in the next few weeks.

~

PENN

I UNLOADED our luggage and supplies and dragged them into the house the council had quickly cleaned for us. All they'd had time for was a quick wipe down. The dust was minimal, the bathroom was clean, and any cobwebs were gone.

The house had three bedrooms, but only the largest bedroom had a bed. I hoped Venus didn't object to sleeping with me. The kitchen had the bare minimum to cook a basic meal, but no food. I had packed plenty.

I shoved my hands in my pockets as I finished taking in the old farmhouse in the middle of the town. It had once been the focus of Garnet River and since the council kept it for Brighton, I guessed it had been in her family for generations. The hardwood floors were original but needed TLC. Exposed wood was faded and dry, but would come alive with the right treatment. Functionality was built into every room, and for an old house, it had an open concept. My place in Silver Lake wasn't much different, but it'd been kept up over the years. This house hadn't.

When I had bought my house, I had wanted to

research the best way to remodel it. I had researched the shit out of it, but that wasn't my thing. I had gotten lost in books and didn't finish the project.

I would have time since I didn't have a job.

My work with Garnet's council today was invigorating. It had been an informative session. They outlined their history, which wasn't long. The town had been here for a little over a hundred years. They could get satellite service, but it was slow. I would research how to get broadband capabilities with speeds light years faster than their old satellites. I could gather information on all the tech schools within a hundred miles so the clan could start sending their people to school. They were in desperate need of skilled trade with updated education instead of relying on information passed from generation to generation.

The whole town needed more access to education, from the elementary level on up. Shifters couldn't commingle in the human world until they'd passed puberty and had learned to control their aggression and emotions.

But the council had faced opposition. The town hadn't wanted to contribute financially, and the hoard Brighton's parents had grown was supposedly with them when they crashed. The gems were never found.

That part of the story was suspicious as hell. I believed in coincidences. These roads wound through thick parts of the woods. Hitting a deer, a moose, or an elk wasn't out of the ordinary. But for it to happen with the top three levels of rulers? And with their treasures? In a desolate area where no one had found them?

Shifters could recover from a lot, but when we were gravely injured long enough, even our abilities gave out.

No, it had to be planned. A long game. Was Camden's family savvy enough to carry out a plan for years?

The front door opened. A flushed and sweaty Venus plowed inside, followed by Brighton.

"Oh, this is nice. You didn't need to be worried." Venus gave her a side-eye. "You wouldn't have needed to be worried even if it was a dump."

Brighton lifted a shoulder, but as she took in the room, her expression turned dejected. "Selma replaced the broken windows, and the roof doesn't leak anymore. The bones are good. We'll get around to remodeling it."

"The house I live in is almost as old as this one. I haven't been able to do a lot of renovations since I bought it either."

The tightness in her expression eased. "I helped Selma with a lot, and I enjoyed it." Tension returned. "They're a lot easier with money to buy adequate supplies. Anyway, what time are we meeting tomorrow?"

Before she and Venus got too far with the planning, I jumped in. "I would like at least a half a day with Brighton and the council to cover the changes I recommend." I shot Brighton a pointed look. "You'll need to be the one to order them. It'll be a change in your dynamic since they raised you, but it's a necessary adjustment for your clan. They advise; you lead. You'll find how empowering it is to make decisions when you have"—I ticked up one finger—"information"—I added a second finger—"and options."

"Information and options," Brighton echoed, nodding, but the move was more for herself. She was learning quickly. She came from a long line of Garnet clan rulers. Her natural leadership instincts were there, but she was gaining the skills to use them.

She lifted her chin, a newfound confidence in her eyes that hadn't been there before she worked with Venus. "I'll train in the morning, and after lunch I'll meet with you and the council. One?" Her expression wavered, like she regretted asking if the time was okay.

I bit back a smile. "One."

She gave Venus a playful punch on the shoulder. "See you bright and early, elder." She disappeared out the door with a giggle.

Venus called after her, "You're going to pay for that, you little whippersnapper." She closed the front door and flipped the dead bolt. "Hanging out with her has made you seem older." Venus chuckled as she undid the band around her hair.

"That girl makes me feel way more than two years older than her."

She shook out her waterfall of blonde hair. The green ends brushed the top of her biceps. "I need to shower, and then I want to hear about your day."

"The towels are threadbare, and I don't think the water heater has more than two minutes of hot water."

I meant my comment to be humorous, but Venus studied me with a solemn stare. "Threadbare towels and no hot water is what I'm used to."

"Then I'll make sure you get used to hot water and fluffy fabric." I closed the distance between us. We were finally alone, not traveling, and nowhere to be until tomorrow morning. The smell of the woods clung to her, melding with her sweet scent until I pictured camping and s'mores. "I might be unemployed, but I've got a nice little hoard. I have a jade that I've been hanging on to for almost a decade. I've never been able to part with it, and now I know why."

"And why is that?" She tried to make it sound flirty, but her vulnerability shone through.

"Because I think it would look good in a silver setting around your finger." If I had the stone with me, I would drop to my knees and propose like humans. Instead, I was in an old house with secondhand furnishings, but I had the female I was in love with. I had everything. I took her hands in mine. This was it. I would get my answer. She still had some time, but this moment was as right as it could be. "Venus, will you be mine?"

Her full lips parted. Astonishment and hope mixed in her expression. "The next thing you're going to tell me is that your stone is an oval shape."

"I wouldn't be lying."

"Oh my god, Penn. How can you be so damn perfect? Looks might not be everything, but you're a total package. Yes, dammit. I'm yours."

Sheer possessiveness made me growl, "Mine."

I yanked her toward me and wedged a leg between hers so I could grab her ass and lift her. She had been working out all day, making her scent stronger. We weren't like humans who needed to wash off the dirt and grit. This was our nature. Raw and carnal.

But she had mentioned a shower and my female got what my female wanted.

Her legs were around my waist while my tongue invaded her mouth. I got us to the bathroom without ramming her back into any corners. Without looking, I flipped on the knob. Cold water wouldn't be an issue. I planned to keep her hot and bothered.

I untangled her legs from around me. When her feet touched the floor, I broke the kiss. "I want my mark on you."

She ripped her shirt off, followed by her black-and-neon-green sports bra. She tapped her fingers on a spot between her neck and collarbone. "I want your mark right here."

That was all I needed to hear. She was mine, and soon everyone would know it. Seams ripped as I tore my clothes off. By the time I was done, she was also naked. I lifted her again and stepped over the lip of the tub into the shower. Fuck the shower curtain. I'd clean any mess up later. A spray of lukewarm water cascaded onto us. I didn't consider foreplay a waste, but I wouldn't spare the time. The sweet scent of her arousal filled my nose. I pressed her against the wall and adjusted my hips until the tip of my erection pushed into her welcoming heat.

"Penn," she moaned. Her body was taut around me, locked onto me as if we could become one unit.

I thrust all the way into her and braced my hand on the shower wall by her head. The intensity of our union was staggering. Every time was special, but none would be as crucial as now.

I was claiming my mate. I would lock my teeth into the flesh of her neck and mark her as mine. She was already branded into my soul. Anyone who saw the way I looked at her would know I was hers, but this would make it official in our world.

Everyone already knew I was hopeless for her. She'd been the last one to convince, and goddammit, I'd done it.

I pushed in and out of her, stroking us closer and closer to our peak, ruthlessly efficient. I knew how hard she liked it, and I knew the spot that drove her the wildest. There was no time to play as I carried us to that precipice, the very tip of passion and pleasure, and when we teetered at the very top, I sank my teeth into her tender flesh.

A bite didn't have to be hard, but it was unyielding. My canines just barely punctured her skin. In the old days, claiming was savage, but in today's world, it only needed to be done while we climaxed together, leaving a mark that would soon heal, but not scar.

My name echoed off the walls, and she spasmed around me. As soon as my release hit her tender flesh, our passion ignited. The explosion of my claim ripped through both of us. I held on to her, she held on to me as we moaned and cried through an ecstasy I had never experienced.

The water turned cold. My hair stuck against my head, and hers was plastered against her face. I didn't let her go as I lowered us together into the tub with her on top of me. I shut the water off to give it a chance to heat.

All I wanted to do right now was hold my future mate. "I love you, Venus."

She stroked her fingers up and down my arm. "I tried hard not to, but you're a persistent male. I love you so hard, Penn."

My world finally made sense. Growing up, I had felt lost. I had thrown myself into school. The female that I hadn't dared acknowledge that I wanted had been sworn to my brother. I busied myself another way, not knowing what I would do for a career, or how I could stand to be in Silver Lake and watch him be with her.

But Venus was mine. We would discuss where we made our home, and I would help Garnet River.

"What are you thinking?" she asked.

"That the question of what I was meant to do in this life has finally gotten clear."

She trailed her finger down my neck and chest as if she was gathering all the water droplets. "Other than getting me to submit, what else are you being called to do? Don't you want to teach anymore?"

"I want to teach, but not behind a screen. I want to pass my knowledge on to our people, not a kid whose parents paid for their college, or one who just needs the credit and doesn't care about the subject."

I thought about today and the thrill that filled me from head to toe when the council laid out what they thought was a dismal start to building their future.

"Today was the most fulfilled I felt in my life. The council members actually wanted to hear what I had to say. I rambled, and they didn't stop me. But then, I am a Silver. They kind of had to listen."

She continued her exploration of my body with her fingers. "I have a confession."

I lifted a brow. "Oh?"

"I secretly want you to ramble on about random knowledge. It used to make me feel stupid, but I honestly wanted to hear what you had to say. Because in that deep voice of yours, you could recite computer code and I would be riveted."

I barked out a laugh. "Good thing for both of us I don't know computer code, or I probably would do it. I think what I needed to do was find a practical application for my skills. Rambling is one thing, but utilizing that info is another."

She brushed my hair off my forehead, unconsciously styling the wet strands. "I think Lachlan would like to hear what you have to say about certain subjects regarding Jade Hills. He might even ask you once we're mated. The clan would be more accepting of a Silver butting into our affairs then."

Our lives were coming together. We'd had some hurdles to work through, but she wore my mark. Soon we'd be mated.

"I know we're ten years apart, but you were meant to be mine."

She drew her bottom lip between her teeth and screwed her face up like she was thinking. "I don't know. I feel like you need to prove it some more."

This time, I would prove it through no less than an hour of foreplay.

CHAPTER

EIGHTEEN

enus

TWO WEEKS HAD GONE BY. Our time was wrapping up in Garnet River. I'd worked with Brighton every day. I left it up to her to decide when, and she had surprised me when she changed our times each day. I couldn't have been any prouder. Keeping it random, changing it up. Just how a strategic leader needed to think.

We had even varied our training areas. Some days, we worked out in the same space. Other days, we trained in one area before moving to another. I worked with her in the water, in the trees, and in an open field, everywhere she could possibly get into a fight. Last weekend, we had even done some urban and night training.

Just as I had suspected after the first day working with her, she learned quickly. She had been taught the basics of fighting; it had been the practice she was missing. And we had practiced.

In a couple of days, Steel, Penn, and I leave to go back to Silver Lake and Jade Hills. Penn and I needed to mate before my birthday, and we both wanted to do it closer to home.

Brighton bounced from foot to foot, shadowboxing while she was at it. We had just shifted back from sparring in our dragon forms. Now dressed, we were ready for hand to hand. "Have you decided where you're holding the ceremony?"

I rotated my arms to warm up my shoulders. Dragon shifters healed fast, but that didn't mean I wanted to be sore the rest of the day. And maybe to give us some time before we started. We had gotten used to adding some chitchat to our time together. Precious girl talk I hadn't gotten enough of in my life.

"Jade Hills. He wants my clan to hear his emphatic yes when he says our vows."

"That's sweet. Are all male shifters like him?"

I twisted back and forth at the waist. "Nope." I frowned and paused. "Maybe? Maybe just around their mate."

She stretched her arms above her head. Our time together was ticking away, but I was confident in her ability. She needed the girl talk more right now. "I wonder if I'll ever meet someone out here in the middle of nowhere."

"You never know."

She gave me a droll look. "I kind of do know. I know everyone in a thirty-mile radius, and none of them are mate material. Not for me."

I chuckled. She had a point. I had been here long

enough to meet a lot of the clan. I had gone to the neighboring town with Brighton to pick up groceries with Selma. There weren't many human males around Brighton's age in the vicinity. But she was young yet.

Without warning, I charged her. Her eyes briefly flared, then narrowed. By the time I reached her, she was ready for me. We grappled, her strength straining against mine. I no longer had to hold back. Two and a half weeks of filling her with meat and potatoes and her body's natural healing abilities had filled her out. She'd packed on muscles that should've been there years ago, but they were there now and she knew how to use them.

She flipped me over her shoulder. Before she could pile on top of me, I rolled. I jumped to my feet and froze.

A strange scent filled my nose. Brighton stopped midlaunch and dropped to a crouch, her gaze scanning the woods.

The steady flow of the river was in the distance. But the birds had gone quiet in the trees to my right. The area to my left went silent.

"Back to back," I said under my breath.

We each turned around and circled in our fighting crouch. I inhaled, sifting through the different scents, filtering out rabbits, birds, bugs. The new scent was growing stronger. A male. Wait. A female.

More scents assaulted my nose. There was more than one shifter out there.

"The Millers," Brighton said in a low voice.

That entire family had been conspicuously absent while I was in town. I had almost forgotten about them. A dangerous mistake.

"How many?" I spoke just as quietly. The shifters creeping up on us wouldn't be able to hear what I said.

"There's seven of them. Two parents. Camden's grandfather. Another grandmother, and two siblings, both two years younger than me."

Fuck me sideways and upside down. Seven against two? "Our best chance is with our dragons."

I had never stripped faster in my life. Brighton shed her last article of clothing just as I did. Branches cracked and snapped. They didn't want us shifting.

Too late. I let the change take me over. Heat charged the air behind me as Brighton shifted. She was still smaller than me, but she could fight, and she would have to fight better than she ever had today.

A rifle blast rang out from the trees. Searing agony stabbed into my flank. What dragon shifters used fucking guns?

A question no one had thought to ask—where had the Trevinos gotten their weapons? Ah, hell. Had the Millers been the ones to shoot Steel and Penn? They'd meant to kill whoever dealt with the Trevinos. Steel and Penn had saved Brighton that day.

Brighton jumped to my side as if to make a shield with her dragon form, but I wouldn't allow her to take a round for me. She was the last of her line for Garnet clan. I had two brothers. But another blast rang out. This one from another direction. Then another blast. And another.

We were two dragons in the middle of a large clearing, surrounded by shifters with weapons. The continuous ring of gunfire might be heard in town. Help might come—eventually.

Pain lanced through my body like a lightning storm. I nudged Brighton with my head and silently urged her to go. These woods were private enough she could take to the sky. It was risky in broad daylight, but she could get to safety.

She shook her head and prowled around me. Blood dripped from her tail. A bullet had knocked a few scales from her neck.

I headbutted her again. She was the ruler, but I was older and more experienced, dammit. My vision blurred. Shit. I had to get her out of here before I went down. She couldn't take on seven shifters alone.

I let out a roar and body-slammed her toward the trees where she would be a harder target. The metallic tang of her blood mixed with the cloud of mine in the air. Agony lit my body like a Christmas tree and the only color of lights was pain. I couldn't fly. Our only hope was for her to find help.

My vision went blurry just as another blast echoed through the trees. I slammed her toward the tree line, forcing her to take to the air or break her body against tree trunks.

The recoil of my body was the only way I knew I had been hit. I couldn't tell through the haze of pain clouding my vision.

Brighton let out a roar and soared over the tops of the trees, keeping low, her flight path erratic, whether intentional or from her injuries, I didn't know.

Injured or not, I wasn't going down without a fight. I poured the last of my energy into a mighty roar and stormed into the woods.

≈

PENN

. . .

I RACED out the door and into the middle of the street, spinning in a tight circle to pinpoint where the sound came from. The rest of the council poured out of city hall.

Selma squinted as if that would help her hear better. She pointed in the direction Venus and Brighton had jogged off in this morning. "Over there."

"Are those fucking gunshots?" It wasn't hunting season. So who the fuck was getting shot at?

The spots where I was shot weeks ago throbbed. Rage flooded my veins. Venus couldn't be in trouble. If one inch of her soft skin was damaged, I would rampage.

A dark spot floated above the treetops. The form of a dragon came into view. Her path was erratic as she careened toward town.

"That's Brighton," Selma said, alarm filling her voice. She took off in a run, faster than I'd expected for a shifter her age.

I ran after her. As soon as Brighton bumped down in the middle of the street, she staggered and lurched like a plane that had lost its landing gear. She tumbled to a stop. The scent of her blood filled the air and red stained her neck and her tail. Selma crouched next to her.

I skidded to a stop next to her. "Where's Venus?"

Brighton's large mouth gaped open, and a cry left her as she shifted to her human form. She sagged against the concrete. "The Millers attacked us," she gasped. "I smelled all of them. Venus made me leave to get help."

The glint in Selma's eyes was hot enough to make the trees around town catch fire. She wrapped an arm under Brighton to help her up. "I'll get the others."

I didn't bother to pause and think or plan. I refused to take the time. Taking off at a dead sprint, I ran in the direction Brighton had come from. Shifters stepped out onto the sidewalk, looking around, their gaze landing on Brighton, limp with Selma. Confusion hung in the air.

But I was damn clear about where I was going. Something was wrong with my mate, and I had to find her.

Running through the trees, the scent of several shifters surrounded me. Were they ambushed?

Venus was strong. I hadn't seen her fight, but I didn't have to in order to know that she was good. But I had already sifted through the fresh sense of five shifters—six. No one could take on six shifters. Two against—I parsed a seventh scent. Shit.

I reached the clearing. Blood splattered the grass. Two large pools of red smothered the blades as it soaked into the soil. White chocolate and anguish surrounded me.

Venus was gone.

Where could she be? I tried to follow the scent, but the stench of the other shifters made it hard to separate the trails.

How could they have disappeared with my female so fast?

Blood marred the grass in a path toward a section of the tree line where several branches had been broken. I followed the trail. No Venus. More blood.

I fought the urge to drop to my knees and let out a roar that would shake the surrounding trees. It would do no good.

People crashed through the woods behind me. The council. Maybe some nosy clan members. If they weren't there to help, I didn't care.

I pulled out my phone and dialed Steel.

"Venus and Brighton were attacked. Venus is gone.

Call Deacon and get here ASAP." I let Steel deal with Deacon while I called Venus's brother.

Whoever hurt her would suffer. I would make sure of it. Her brothers would make sure of it. When Lachlan answered, I repeated the same thing.

"Ronan and I are on the way," was all he said before he hung up.

Grateful I wasn't burdened with questions and explanations, I hung up and faced the growing crowd behind me.

My chest heaved as I peeled off my shirt. "If you aren't here to look for Venus and terminate the attackers, then get the fuck out of my way. All those involved will die. This is your only warning."

Brighton stepped out from behind two of the younger council members. She hadn't given herself time to heal. "I'll shift and search the Millers' property with Selma and the others." She pointed to a group of three females not much older than her. "You three follow the river. Look for tracks. They might've taken a boat to escape. We hunt as dragons. They used guns against their own kind. I order their death."

Selma began undressing, as did the other three council members. "Go in groups, protect each other. The Millers are avid hunters."

Too late now, I realized we hadn't looked for rifles at the Trevinos'. I'd worry about that after they were dead.

I wasn't worried about hunting in a group. I jerked my clothing off and shifted. Bones stretched, muscles lengthened, and I grew bigger. I embraced the change and the power flooding my body. I would find my mate and I didn't care what land I had to raze when I did it.

Without bothering to see if anyone was joining me, I

continued searching for the white chocolate scent. In this form, sounds and smells were more acute. The silver sheen from being one of the Silver ruling family covered the natural green of dragon shifters, lending well to a natural camouflage. Shadows dusted over my scales as I swung my mighty head around, sniffing the air.

The splatter spread out after several yards, and trees crowded around me. She had either bled less at this point, or they were running with her. The latter made sense. For them to have disappeared so quickly before I got here, they'd had a plan.

That was when I smelled the stench of exhaust in the air. Up ahead, the grass was crushed into parallel lines. A four-wheeler.

I chased the imprints as far as I could. The benefit of an ATV in the trees meant that the path it took was wider than one a shifter needed to travel on foot. I propelled down the trail, limbs banging against my scales like angry gnats on a summer night. I wasn't stopping until I found my female.

The trees grew thinner, and other smells of exhaust mixed in the air. I barreled onto a dirt road. I recognized this area. Steel and I had driven through here to get to the Trevinos'.

Looking behind me showed no one had followed me. Either I had gone too fast, or they had spread out. There were a lot of woods to cover.

Racking my brain, I struggled to remember the layout of Garnet land from my meetings with the council. A mental map formed in my mind. They owned a lot of the surrounding area. Acres with their homes. More land for their mechanic shop.

Their property would be nothing but splinters by the time I was done.

Turning side to side, I sniffed the air and listened hard. The lingering fumes smelled fresher to my right, which would take me to the edges of their land.

I spun around and ducked back into the trees. It was time for stealth. It was time to prove my students were right. Looks weren't everything and my brains only carried me so far. I was a dragon shifter and I could fight like a beast.

CHAPTER
NINETEEN

enus

I KEPT AN EYELID CRACKED. The move took all my energy. I couldn't believe I had any blood left, but that was the curse of the healing ability. I would keep healing enough to keep myself alive, lost in a perpetual state of regeneration until my energy faded slowly to nothing. Then I would die.

Was this how Brighton's family perished? Help was withheld until they'd all succumbed to their injuries?

How much had the Millers planned? Or had they been adept at taking advantage of certain situations? Like the Trevinos and Brighton's hesitance at dealing with them? The stench on the Trevinos' property would've hidden their presence.

It was all so crystal fucking clear now. And I couldn't do a damn thing about it.

Two older shifters and the two youngest had hauled me away. After being unceremoniously bounced and bumped through the woods, I didn't mind the musty wooden floor I was tossed against.

Like the Trevinos had done with Steel and Penn, I had a large bowie knife shoved into my side. Getting shot was its own special hell, but adding a blade wedged between my scales through a vulnerable part of my chest was a new level.

Two things kept me going. I fantasized about slowly ripping the limbs off the four shifters who had taken me, and I worried about what Penn was going through.

The shifters who'd taken me had to know Penn would look for me. They had to know Deacon and Steel were still in the city and would come for me.

If they knew.

Did Brighton make it to town?

I had thrashed in the trees, ready to rain death, but the extent of my blood loss had made me pass out.

Real fearsome, Venus.

Had anyone heard the gunfire? My roar?

I didn't know what time it was, but I could safely estimate it had been long enough that people were looking for me.

Two of the other shifters posted watch over me. They had rotated out once already. One elder with one of the younger shifters.

I had been roaming in and out of consciousness when we had arrived at this place. The floor was musty, but I didn't get the sense it was underground. My senses were dulled thanks to my injuries, but I caught whiffs of oil and gasoline. A shed? No, it had to be big enough for a dragon. I hadn't been able to shift thanks to the pain.

196

So, a sizable structure. Perhaps a shop, maybe where their mechanic shop was. If they dominated engine repair for the clan, they might have more than one place.

I strongly suspected before, but now I didn't doubt the Millers were behind the accident that wiped out Brighton's family. Maybe I was giving them too much credit, but minds like that didn't dwell on causing harm to others. It came naturally. I had witnessed enough of it in my lifetime.

"Why don't we just kill her?" the younger shifter hissed.

"Because you fucked up and shot too early. Pretty fucking hard to make this look like an accident, so now we need leverage." Boots scraped on the floor as the older male adjusted his seat. "They know it was us and she's from a ruling family."

I couldn't see the young male reply, but I heard the fear in his voice. "They can fucking try. I'm not scared of no Envy."

"That's the thing, Will. You're still calling them Envies. Have you heard of this one getting jealous and rampaging in the last few weeks? Her and her brothers ain't like her parents. And she's with a Silver. Camden might've gotten us all killed," the older shifter ended with a mutter.

The older male was still in the enemy category, but I appreciated his insight.

"Camden knows what he's doing." Adoration rang from Will's voice through the shop. He might not hold a specific grudge against me, but his big brother did, and that was all that mattered. This kid wasn't a kid. He was close to Brighton's age, but he hadn't learned to think for himself. If he'd been the one to shoot me like the older guy said, then he also craved violence, but was too chickenshit to face me as a shifter.

Fatigue swamped me like a wet wool blanket. My energy was fading. I didn't know how much longer I could last.

My eyelids drifted shut. I should conserve energy. Just for a little bit.

I pried them open. No. I couldn't succumb. But as drop after drop of blood leaked out of me, I wasn't certain how much longer I could last.

I had to force my brain to work. If these two were going to chitchat, then I had to think about something intriguing enough to keep me conscious. If I was in a shop, was there another room the other two shifters were in? Where were the rest?

My heart rate kicked up when I thought they may have gotten to Brighton. I had to hope for the best and preserve my energy.

"How much longer until Jess and Grandma get back?" The younger shifter sounded like a petulant child. Ronan could've turned out like him. The oldest sibling got all the attention, but had also absorbed the worst of the tough love. But Ronan was nothing like this guy.

"Another hour."

Will let out a long groan. Chair legs scraped against the floor before footsteps padded back and forth. Will was restless. "It's almost eight. Are we going to do this all night?"

Eight? It had been shortly after lunch when I was attacked. Had over seven hours gone by? I had passed out for longer lengths of time than I thought.

That didn't bode well for me. My eyelids grew heavy. I was on my side and could see little more than grains of dirt littering the concrete floor, but I had to continue studying each piece of debris. My life depended on it.

"We're going to do this as long as we have to do this." The grandpa's voice was steady.

"We're going to get executed for this, you know. We should kill her and get what satisfaction we can."

"Will," the grandpa snapped. "The Silvers are powerful, but we outnumber them. Our runt of a ruler can't take us. And if this Envy's brothers even bother to come this far, we'll kill them too. Three clans, one coup."

"I want to control Jade. My clan will be the envy of the shifter world. Jess can have fucking Garnet for all the good that's left here."

I wanted to snort, but couldn't spare the effort. The Millers had it all planned. Camden thought he could replace Deacon. Did he think the clans wouldn't retaliate? Penn and Steel were as well liked as their brother. For once, my family was on the side of the good guys.

Yet here I was, bleeding out.

My brothers would bother. They'd rip Garnet River to shreds just like they did to the bullies on the playground. We had wasted our adult lives existing around each other, damaged from how our parents raised us. My conversations with Lachlan had shown me that there was more substance to my brothers than I had imagined.

I wanted to get to know them better. I even wanted to hear their sarcastic comments about the age difference between me and Penn. In those rare moments, I witnessed the humor we had been afraid to express growing up. A trait I had thought originated from a place of cruelty, but it was how we showed we cared. As fucked up as it was, that was Jade. Not perfect, but a hell of a lot better than previous generations.

And I wouldn't let some ambitious twat ruin it.

I had a mate I wanted to spend my life with. I had been claimed, and I hadn't even gotten to flaunt it around Jade Hills. Pushing against the floor, I envisioned eviscerating my two guards. I wasn't going down without a fight. This ended now.

A scuffling of shoes and the rustle of clothing told me the other shifters were up and ready for me. But they were in human form.

I continued to strain, but I couldn't even lift my heavy body an inch off the ground. My limbs shook. Fire wicked up and down my body. Instead of struggling to rise, I was fighting not to collapse.

This wasn't going the way I wanted it to.

I didn't know which one slammed a boot into my tender belly, but I gagged out a croak. I didn't even have the energy to roar.

My muscles gave out. I slumped to the floor. I anticipated another kick. Will was itching to kill me, but I was left alone to fight the lure of unconsciousness.

"Did you hear that?" the older male said.

An angry bellow preceded a slam against the building. Dust shook from the rafters. Another slam. Wood splintered and moonlight spilled through the space. As screams and shrieks filled the air, I caught a tantalizing scent against the new cloying cloud of blood.

My mate had arrived.

My lips were working, trying to say his name. He was here. He had found me.

I just didn't know if it was in time to save me.

~

Penn

THE SMELL of her blood enraged me. I'd grown up being told how smart I was, how I was the laid-back brother, the brother without a care in the world. Seeing my female bleeding out on a dirty floor with a knife wedged between her gorgeous scales turned me into an unthinking beast.

I had ripped the two shifters apart. Their heads had rolled away from their bodies and limbs scattered the floor. There would be no coming back from that, no healing for them. They paid for what they had done to her. Just like the other two I had found a few miles away heading here.

The green sheen to her scales was dull. I rushed to her side, shifting as I went. An eyelid was cracked open, but she wasn't seeing anything. I was losing her.

I yanked the knife out like she had done for me in the cellar of the Trevinos' house. Then I sank to the floor and lifted her cool head into my lap. I didn't have Deacon's ability. I couldn't share my healing energy, but I refused to leave. There was no help to be found. There were no doctors for dragon shifters.

"You're strong," I murmured. "Stay with me, V. I love you."

The tiniest puff came out of her snout, but it wasn't exactly a rally. She was weak and had used copious amounts of energy to stay alive.

Stroking my hands over her smooth scales, I talked. About everything and nothing. I told her about Raleigh scattering and how it makes the sky blue. And how I chose biology because it covered a little of everything and might be the most useful subject for the area we lived in. I even confessed that I had studied so hard to keep my mind off her.

I even told her the story I hadn't told anyone. A silly tale that my brothers would've given me shit until they were old and brittle and could barely talk. "I got poison ivy on my privates, V. I was supposed to collect leaves from a hundred different types of trees, and I was determined to get the most variety. I could never be like the other students. We might heal quickly, but let me tell you —poison ivy sticks around. And it doesn't take much burning before healing feels like eternity."

I stroked her graceful neck. Was she colder than before? Panic clawed into my throat. She was mine. She was finally mine. I couldn't lose her. "Hang in there, V. I'll be here until you get up."

I sensed my brothers before I heard them. "In here," I croaked, my throat clogged with worry and fear.

Deacon charged into the shop, barely sparing a glance for the massive bloodshed and body parts lying around. Steel rushed in behind him.

"Can you help her?" He had healed Ava's father once, but he was human. Would Deacon be able to do anything for the massive injuries Venus had sustained?

I couldn't look at him. I couldn't see if there was defeat in his eyes when he took in my mate. He kneeled by her stomach, holding his hands over her and concentrating on one green scale.

The beautiful dragon that had ravaged the cellar like an avenging angel had lost her luster. The jade sheen of her clan was faint under Deacon's hands.

Steel crouched beside me, giving my shoulder a squeeze. "Her brothers stayed with Brighton to hunt

202

Camden and his parents. Deacon and I felt like we had to find you."

Shifters weren't psychic, but as brothers, we were close. I was grateful for the connection we had. Deacon might not have made it in time. I wasn't sure I had.

Strain etched into Deacon's features as he focused his energy on her.

"Is it working?" I couldn't bring myself to ask the last part of that question—is she too far gone? According to Steel, Ava's dad had been as close to dead as a human could get, but Venus was a dragon shifter. Her injuries might be too grave to come back from.

Deacon dropped to his ass and draped his arms over his knees. His face was pale, wan, as he took in the still form of Venus. "Now we wait. I stemmed the bleeding and gave her every spare drop of energy I could. Let me recoup for a few minutes and I'll do it again."

I nodded, wishing he could keep at it. I hated being this conflicted, a part of me wanting my brother to destroy himself to save my mate, but he was being strategic. He was doling out his supply, recovering, and then he'd attempt again.

Hours ticked by. Venus didn't get worse, but she wasn't getting better. Her own energy wasn't bouncing back, however slowly.

The scent of new shifter rivals made me bare my teeth even though I was in my human form. Two blond males piled through the doorway. Lachlan and Ronan. Brighton was behind them. All three were naked from shifting and covered in blood. I hoped it was the blood of the Millers I didn't kill.

"I'd ask what the hell happened here, but the story is

written in blood," Ronan said, rage barely suppressed in his voice.

Lachlan was a natural-born leader. He might have the same ability as Deacon.

"Can you help her?" I asked. "Deacon's keeping her alive, but we need more."

Lachlan had always been a serious male, but if I had to hang my hopes on his expression, I would give up and walk out into the night, never to return. He circled around us and crouched on the other side of Venus across from Deacon. "I've only done this once before."

"It comes naturally." Deacon pressed his hands against Venus's ragged belly. "Just don't deplete yourself too much. I don't want to fight your sister about letting you die."

The leaders concentrated while the rest of us were relegated to moral support. Steel remained next to me. Ronan and Brighton crouched by Lachlan, their bodies tense like they were ready to jump in and help where needed.

"Enough." Deacon fisted his hands and hung his head. Lachlan continued, his fingers spread, white from the effort. "Lachlan. You can't help her if you drain all of your energy."

Lachlan's green eyes blazed. "I've killed for her before, and I'll do it again."

The three of us stared at him. No one had expected a shocking revelation. It wasn't Silver clan's job to know everything about the other clans, but we oversaw them. Deacon was expected to know the highlights, and knowing who the other rulers were killing was a definite priority.

"Lachlan," Deacon said in a gentler tone, as if he

sensed yelling and ordering wouldn't get through to the other male. "She needs you strong. This is going to be a long process. But we can do it if you listen to me."

The glow in Lachlan's emerald eyes dimmed, and he fisted his hands. His jaw was a granite slab as he studied his sister.

Ronan laid his hands by the bony armor running down her back. "She is strong. She's lasted this long; she'll make it through healing."

I brushed my hand down her long neck. "She's warmer," I murmured. That had to be a good sign.

"Are the rest dead?" I wouldn't leave Venus, but that didn't stop my bloodlust.

"Camden got away," Brighton growled, the red in her eyes catching the moonlight pouring through the garage door I busted down. "I got a chunk of him, but he's disappeared."

"We tracked him for miles," Ronan answered. "Little fucker's wily. But he's alone. The rest of his family is dead."

"He is mine to hunt." Command filled Brighton's voice. "I will end him and get back the control he's tried to steal from me. I will make him pay for my family, for your family, and for Venus. The male will suffer, this I promise."

The gravity of Brighton's vow was lost on none of us, but we'd all swear the same in her position.

Lachlan's approving nod matched Deacon's. "That male is not prepared for the small one's wrath. He was too arrogant. People like that think their cruelty will carry them through, that it makes them impenetrable. He's learned now, but you'll always be able to get him through his arrogance."

Ronan absently patted his sister's side like he was trying to give her unspoken reassurance. "I will be watching, Garnet. I will hold you to your promise."

"You do that, Jade," Brighton snapped.

I concentrated on the prone dragon. Venus was my only concern, but I didn't want her to recover only to continue to be in danger.

"When do we try again?" Lachlan asked.

Wariness hung over Deacon's powerful frame, but he held his hands out. It was too soon, but I doubted Lachlan would wait, and apparently Deacon agreed.

This time, when they funneled their energy into my mate, she let out a long groan. Her form began to shift, scales melted into skin as her body shrunk into her human form. Lachlan let out a relieved sigh and shoved both his hands through his hair.

"Just like her," Ronan muttered. "Stubbornly taking her time."

I lifted a bloodied Venus into my arms. She wouldn't recover on dirty concrete. I planned to carry her through the woods into town until we got to the little borrowed house, and then we were going to sit under the mediocre spray of the shower until all the blood washed away and she was completely healed.

CHAPTER
TWENTY

enus

I STOOD across from the handsome male who was now my mate. I had found a simple white cocktail dress with a green belt and Penn wore an outfit similar to the one he'd worn on our date night.

We had just completed our ceremony in Garnet River city hall. My brother had performed the ceremony with Deacon on one side and Brighton on the other. Ava stood with Steel and Ronan and Garnet River's council as our audience. I missed Avril, but as a human, she couldn't take part in our mating ceremonies unless she was part of the clan. Our vows would be hard to explain to a human.

Penn's eyes were a vivid ocean blue and his smile had only gotten wider after we said our vows.

I had wanted to mate Penn in Jade Hills, but rubbing my mating in the face of all the naysayers in my clan had taken a back seat to my impending birthday. I wasn't risking wasting any more time. Penn had said nothing, but he had been unconsciously looking toward the horizon as if the countdown to my thirty-fifth birthday echoed in the background.

But this ceremony was fitting. Everyone I cared about surrounded me, save my favorite clients. I'd throw a separate celebration with them. I would have plenty of time. Penn was moving to Jade Hills. He'd sell his house in Silver Lake and work on his new business from my house.

Brighton gave me a hug. She still looked terribly young, but there was wisdom in her gaze where uncertainty had lingered before. Confidence had infused her posture and her actions since the night she had tracked down Camden.

I couldn't stay and help her train for her eventual fight with Camden, but I didn't doubt she'd become more of a force than she already was.

When I left, Ronan and Lachlan would leave too. Until then, Ronan challenged her newfound security. The poor girl was clearly uncomfortable around my beautiful brother, but she refused to back down. She put up with his presence for me.

I'd nearly lost my life, but I woke in my mate's arms, surrounded by his cedar, sandalwood, and coriander scent, with family and friends camped outside and in city hall. Friends. Two months ago, I'd felt like I had none. Fitting they were all younger than me—Ava, Avril, Brighton, and, of course, my mate. But their age made sense too, in a way. I'd had my youth stolen from me. I'd hidden within my clan through my twenties. It was time to live. The younger generation treated me based on how I acted, not by the example my parents had set. The older generations were learning—Lachlan, Ronan, and I would make sure of it.

Ava and Brighton gave me a hug before wandering to the table of food the council insisted on providing. Food that had been easier to buy after they'd located the hoard stolen from Brighton's family in the basement of Camden's parents' house.

The young ruler now had a nice hoard to use for herself and her clan.

"Thank you." Deacon and Steel both gave me quick hugs, then turned to Penn.

While Penn's brothers congratulated him, I folded Ronan into a hug. He stiffened, unused to affection, but relaxed after a moment.

"You're getting sappy in your old age." He smiled, but his throat worked like he was fighting back a swell of emotion.

"I'm going to start a new trend, little brother. It's called affection."

He gave an exaggerated shiver. "Consider me warned."

Lachlan was next. I murmured in his ear, "Penn told me what you said in that shop."

He didn't clarify what I'd heard. Guilt mixed with determination in his expression. "I don't need to bother you with the details. It's your mating day."

"I'll let you off today, dear brother. But someday, I'd like the story." I released him and rested my hand on his upper arm. "When you're ready to tell it."

He swallowed hard and averted his gaze. If I thought hard, I could come up with names of who his victims were. Shifters who had wanted to hurt me. But two names topped the list, and if Lachlan had been behind our parents' deaths, I owed him everything. And I didn't need an explanation.

A strong arm wrapped around my waist and tucked me into his side. "Is it bad manners to skip the party and whisk you away?"

"Probably. But maybe if we wait until everyone's busy eating, it won't be so obvious."

"Did you know that in ancient mountain lion shifter mating ceremonies, they used to consummate the mating in front of an audience? That way, it was undisputed. A local witch would be tasked with tracking the date and if the union resulted in young, then she would be used as a witness to confirm the young were the male's?" He grimaced. "Probably not the topic you want to hear on our mating day."

Laughing, I circled my arms around him. When I had come to after Lachlan and Deacon healed me, Penn was cradling me in the bed. He'd showered me and dried me and held me until I finished recovering. And he had talked the whole time he'd been holding me. I had been tempted to pretend to sleep for another few hours, to sink into the well of his voice and enjoy the way random information dripped from his lips. But I'd had other plans for his mouth.

"You can tell me all about it when you're buried deep inside me. Because the longer I'm around you, the more I like when you're a steady stream of loosely associated information. You'll have to tell me the specifics about how our kind can still suffer from poison ivy in our privates."

A faint brush of pink dusted his cheeks. "I was hoping you didn't remember that. Not my finest hour—but the longest."

"I think that story kept me going more than anything you said."

He was midlaugh when Deacon clamped a hand on his shoulder. "Hate to interrupt. I know you're planning to sneak off. I sent your plans to the council. We have their full support, as I expected."

Delight spread across Penn's face and he looked like the geeky twenty-five-year-old I fell in love with. He was creating an online teaching program that all the clans could participate in, especially the more rural ones like Garnet River. It was optional, but I was sure even the most resistant clans would come around.

"I can't wait to start." He rubbed his hand up and down my shoulder. "But it's going to have to wait till after my honeymoon."

Deacon chuckled. "I don't think that will surprise anyone."

While we had lain together, recovering and reconnecting after the rescue, he had asked for ideas about how to be more fun.

I didn't think I'd ever get used to Penn Silver asking me for advice. So, yeah. I had ideas from my experience and years of listening to moms and grandmas discuss their kids and issues with shifter schools. We'd spent hours brainstorming. He had even recruited me to help teach in between my regular work.

The kid who'd gotten made fun of in school was going to teach young shifters. And the guy who'd gotten fired for being too boring was going to inspire new generations. We were an unlikely pair, but we were perfect together.

. . .

———

STEEL GETS some shocking news about his time in the city in The Dragon's Vow.

FOR NEW RELEASE UPDATES, chapter sneak peeks, and exclusive quarterly short stories, sign up for Marie's newsletter and receive my first wolf shifter story free.

THANK YOU FOR READING. I'd love to know what you thought. Please consider leaving a review for The Dragon's Promise at the retailer the book was purchased from.

About the Author

Marie Johnston writes paranormal and contemporary romance and has collected several awards in both genres. Before she was a writer, she was a microbiologist. Depending on the situation, she can be oddly unconcerned about germs or weirdly phobic. She's also a licensed medical technician and has worked as a public health microbiologist and as a lab tech in hospital and clinic labs. Marie's been a volunteer EMT, a college instructor, a security guard, a phlebotomist, a hotel clerk, and a coffee pourer in a bingo hall. All fodder for a writer!! She has four kids, an old cat, and a puppy that's bigger than half her kids.

mariejohnstonwriter.com

Follow me:

Also by Marie Johnston

More in this series

The Dragon's Oath

The Dragon's Promise

The Dragon's Vow

Jade Dragon Shifter Brothers

The Dragon's Pledge

Want to try my very first shifter series?

The Sigma Menace

Fever Claim (Book 1)

Primal Claim (Book 2)

True Claim (Book 3)

Reclaim (Book 3.5)

Lawful Claim (Book 4)

Pure Claim (Book 5)

Printed in Great Britain
by Amazon